JAKE MADDOX
GRAPHIC NOVELS

SOCCER SWITCH

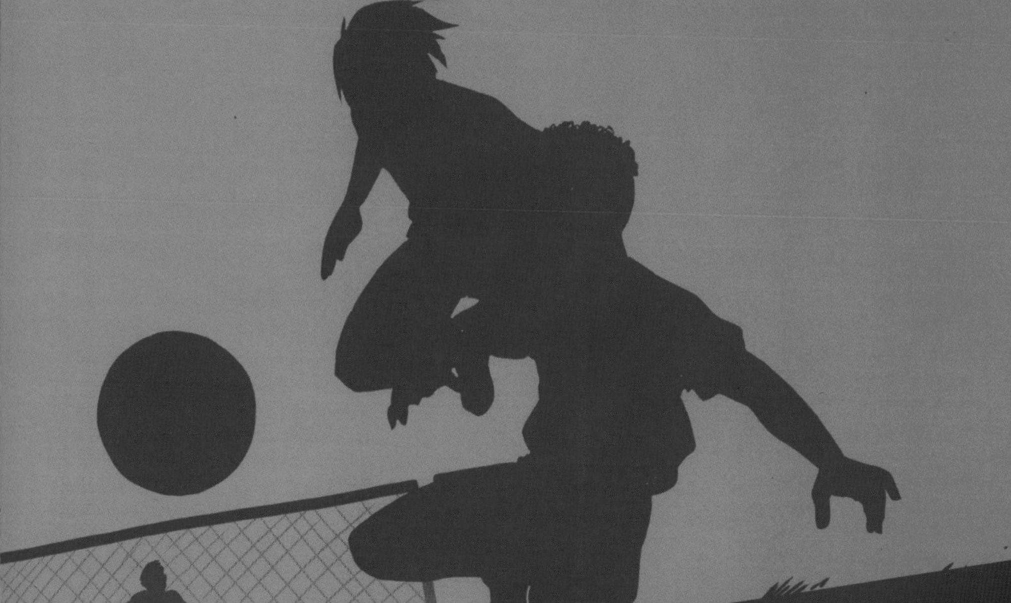

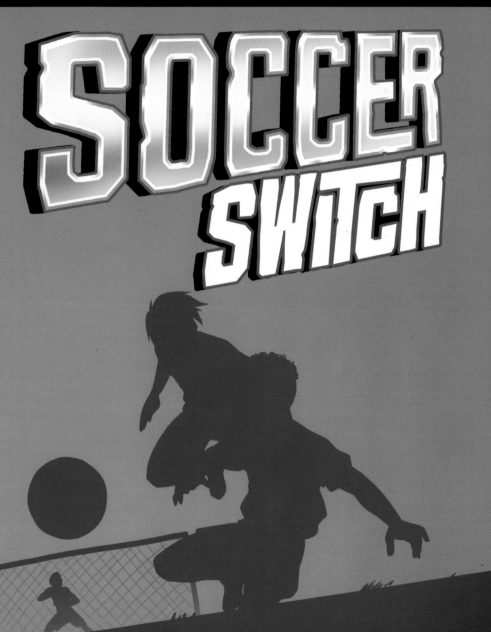

STONE ARCH BOOKS
a capstone imprint

JAKE MADDOX
GRAPHIC NOVELS

Jake Maddox Graphic Novels are published by
Stone Arch Books, a Capstone imprint
1710 Roe Crest Drive
North Mankato, Minnesota 56003

www.mycapstone.com

Library of Congress Cataloging-in-Publication Data is available on the Library of Congress website.

ISBN: 978-1-4965-3699-0 (library binding)
ISBN: 978-1-4965-3703-4 (paperback)
ISBN: 978-1-4965-3719-5 (ebook PDF)

Summary: Andre Makuza is excited for another championship season with his middle school summer soccer team. But a new coach is taking over, and his unusual training methods have the team feeling frustrated. Will the coach's oddball ways ever lead to victory, or is the soccer switch too much for Andre and his teammates to handle?

Editor: Abby Huff
Designer: Brann Garvey
Production: Gene Bentdahl

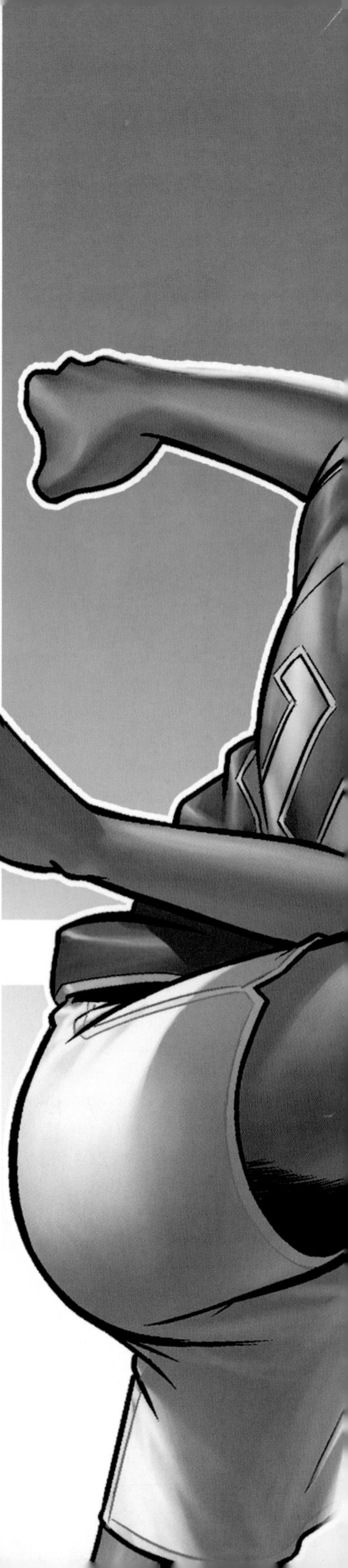

Printed in the United States of America.
010044S17

SOCCER SWITCH

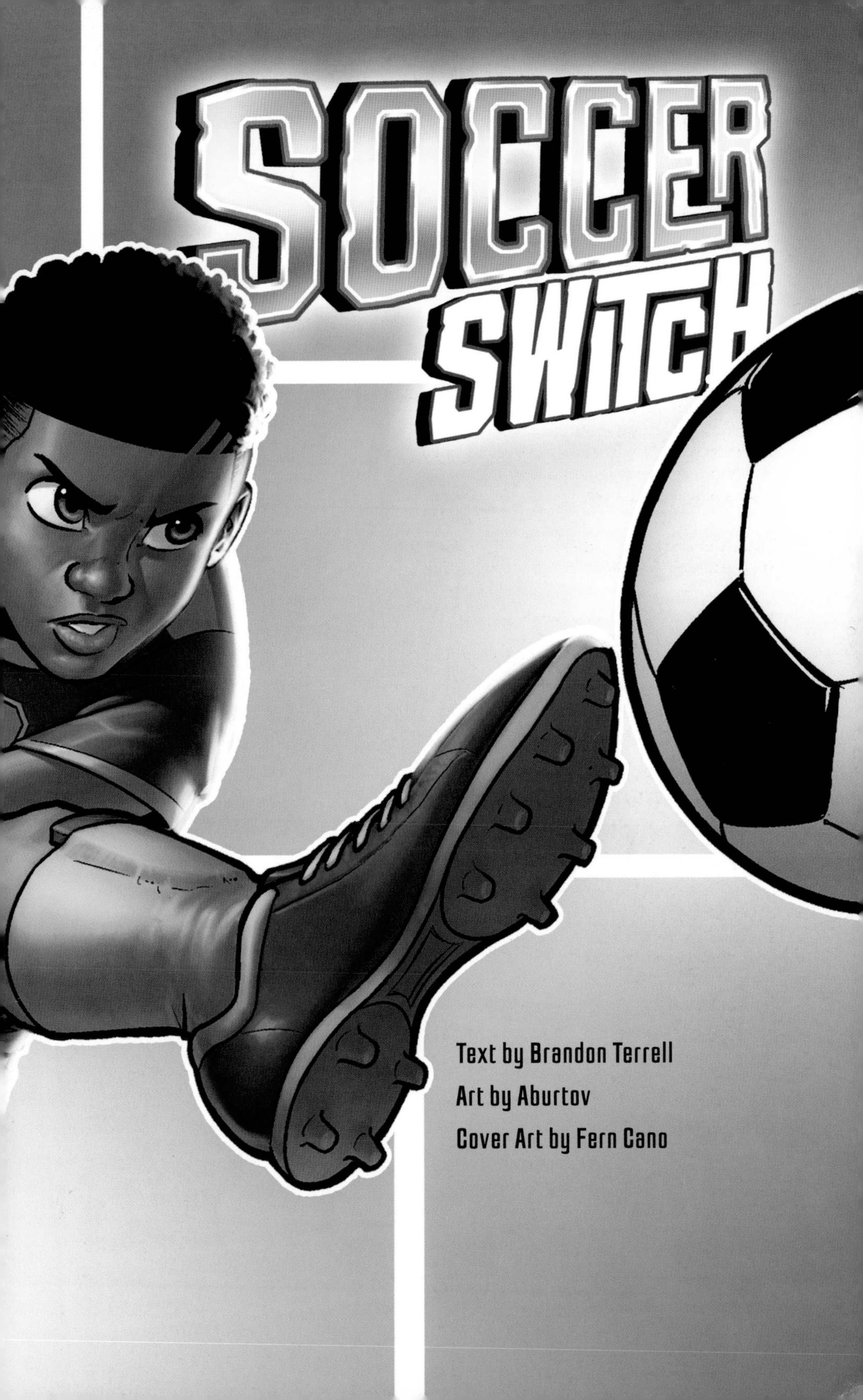

Text by Brandon Terrell

Art by Aburtov

Cover Art by Fern Cano

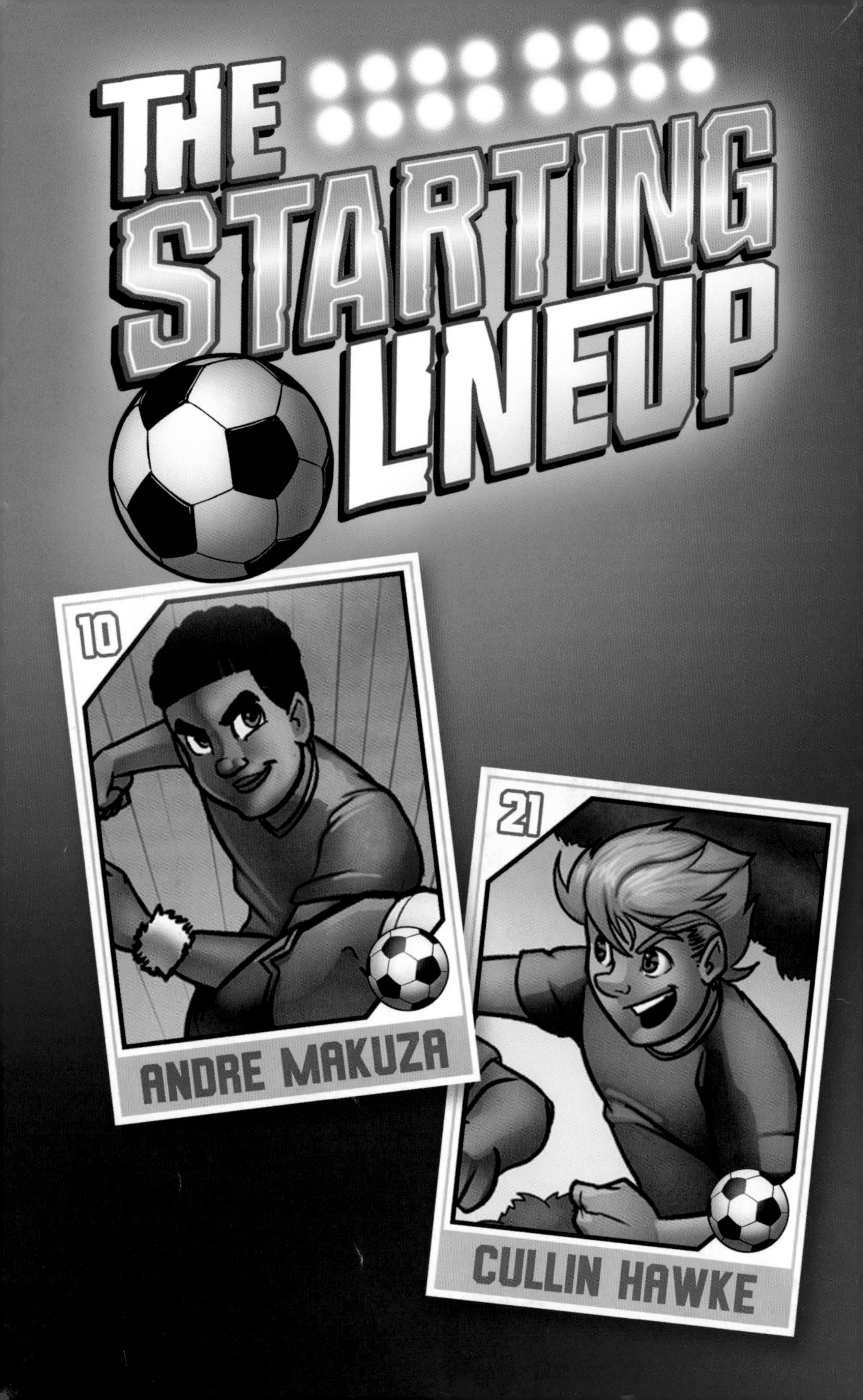
THE STARTING LINEUP
10
ANDRE MAKUZA
21
CULLIN HAWKE

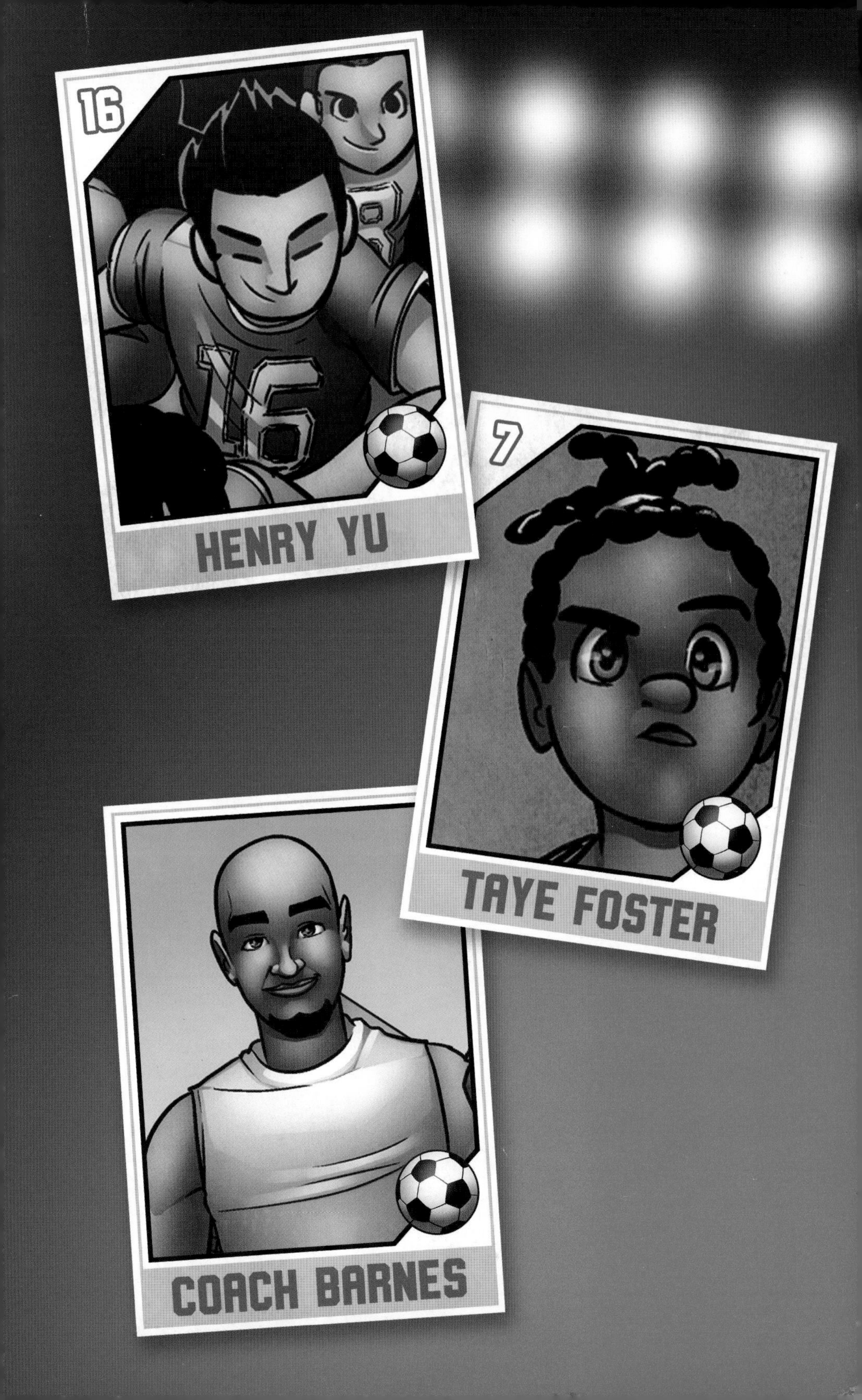
16
HENRY YU
7
TAYE FOSTER
COACH BARNES

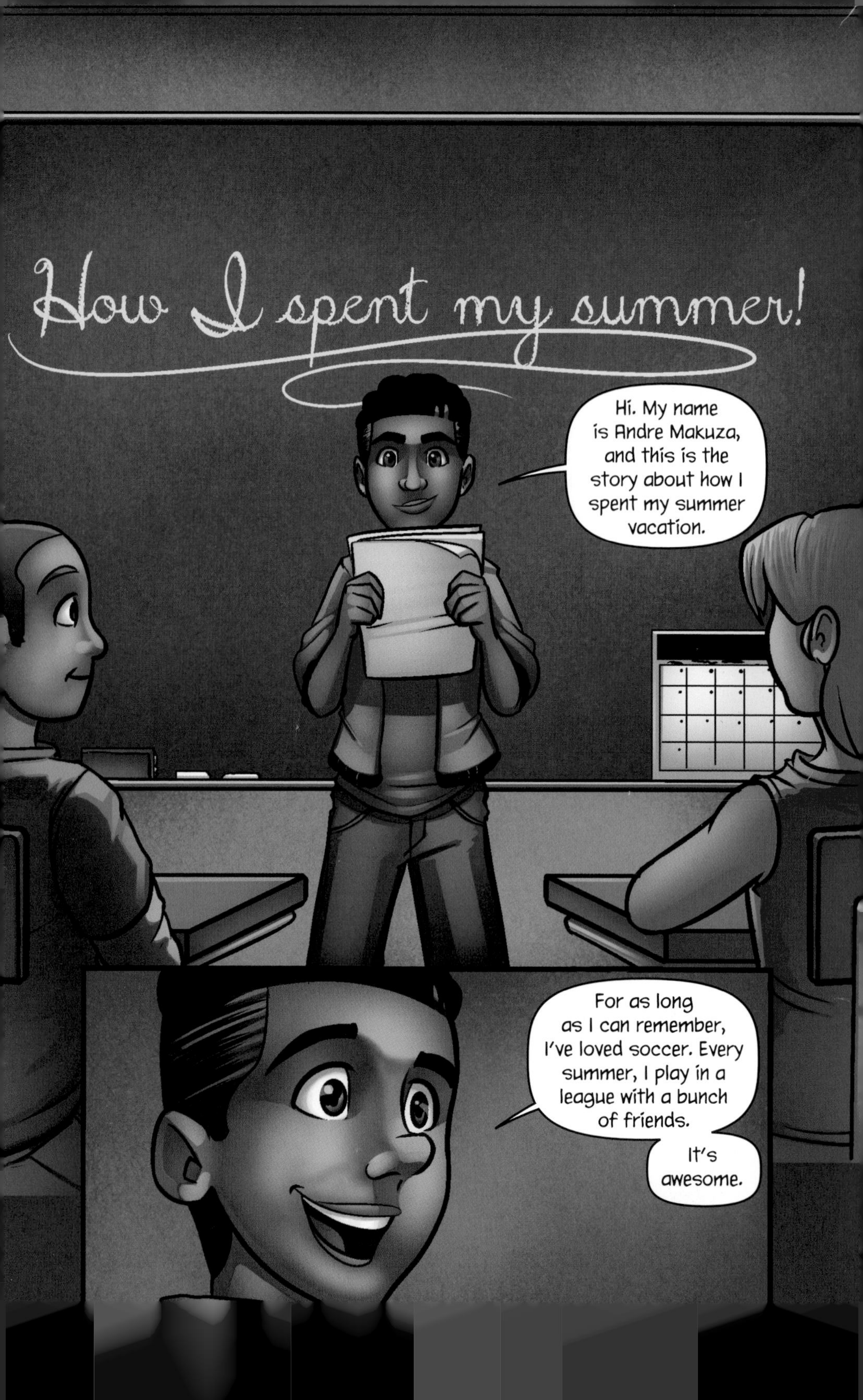
How I spent my summer!
Hi. My name is Andre Makuza, and this is the story about how I spent my summer vacation.
For as long as I can remember, I've loved soccer. Every summer, I play in a league with a bunch of friends.
It's awesome.

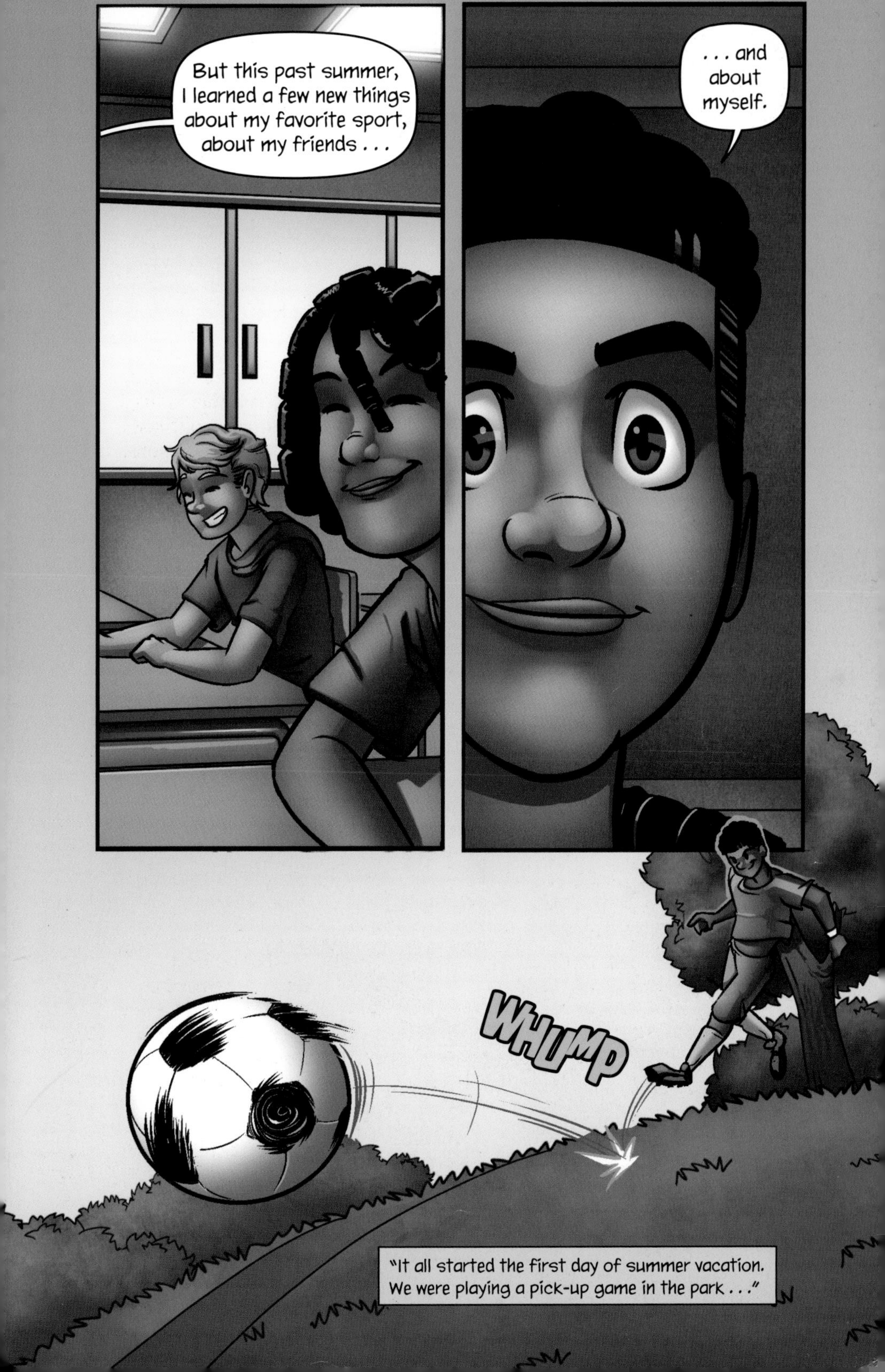
But this past summer, I learned a few new things about my favorite sport, about my friends . . .
. . . and about myself.
WHUMP
"It all started the first day of summer vacation. We were playing a pick-up game in the park . . ."

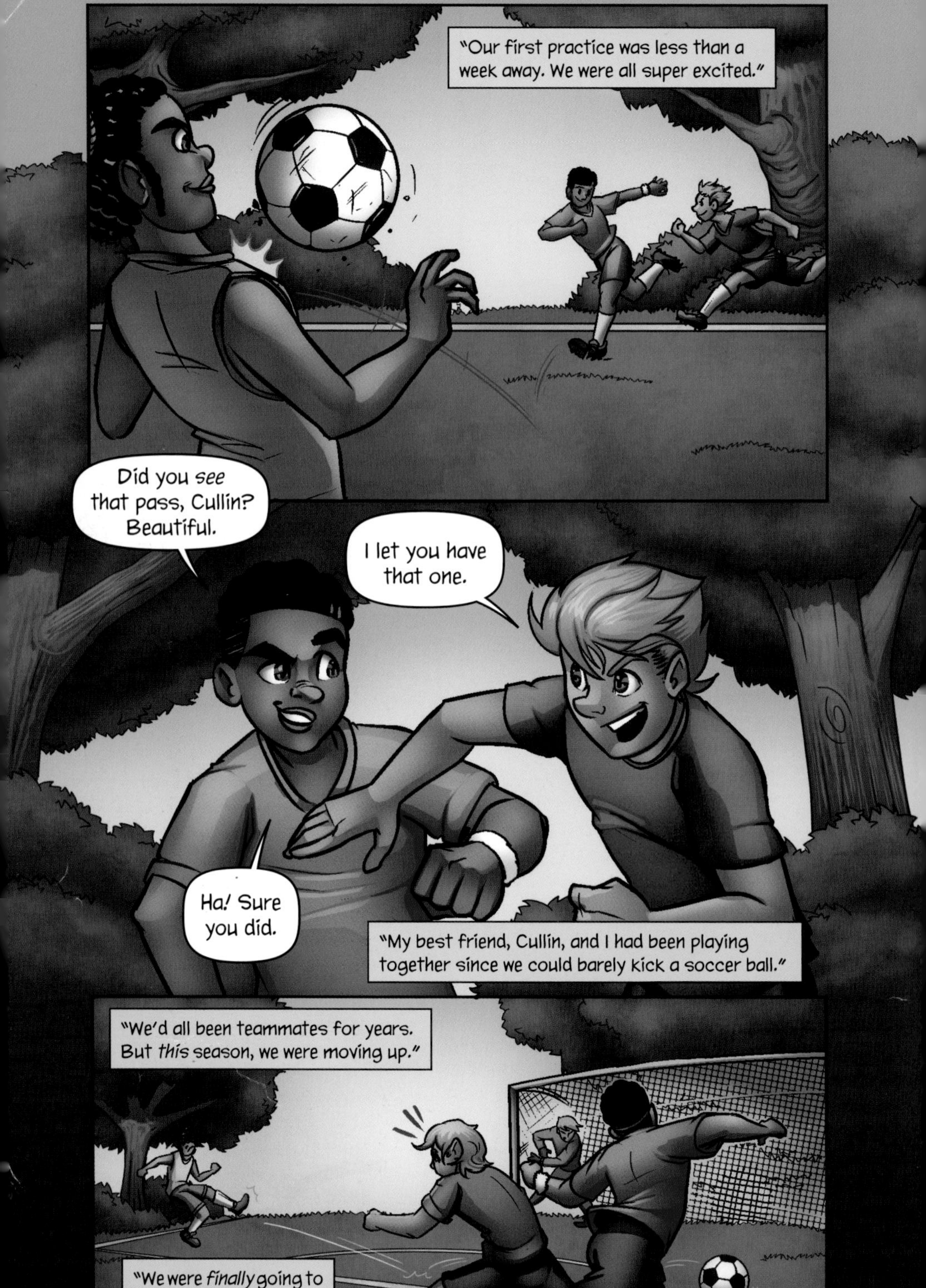
"Our first practice was less than a week away. We were all super excited."
Did you *see* that pass, Cullin? Beautiful.
I let you have that one.
Ha! Sure you did.
"My best friend, Cullin, and I had been playing together since we could barely kick a soccer ball."
"We'd all been teammates for years. But *this* season, we were moving up."
"We were *finally* going to be Mighty Bobcats."

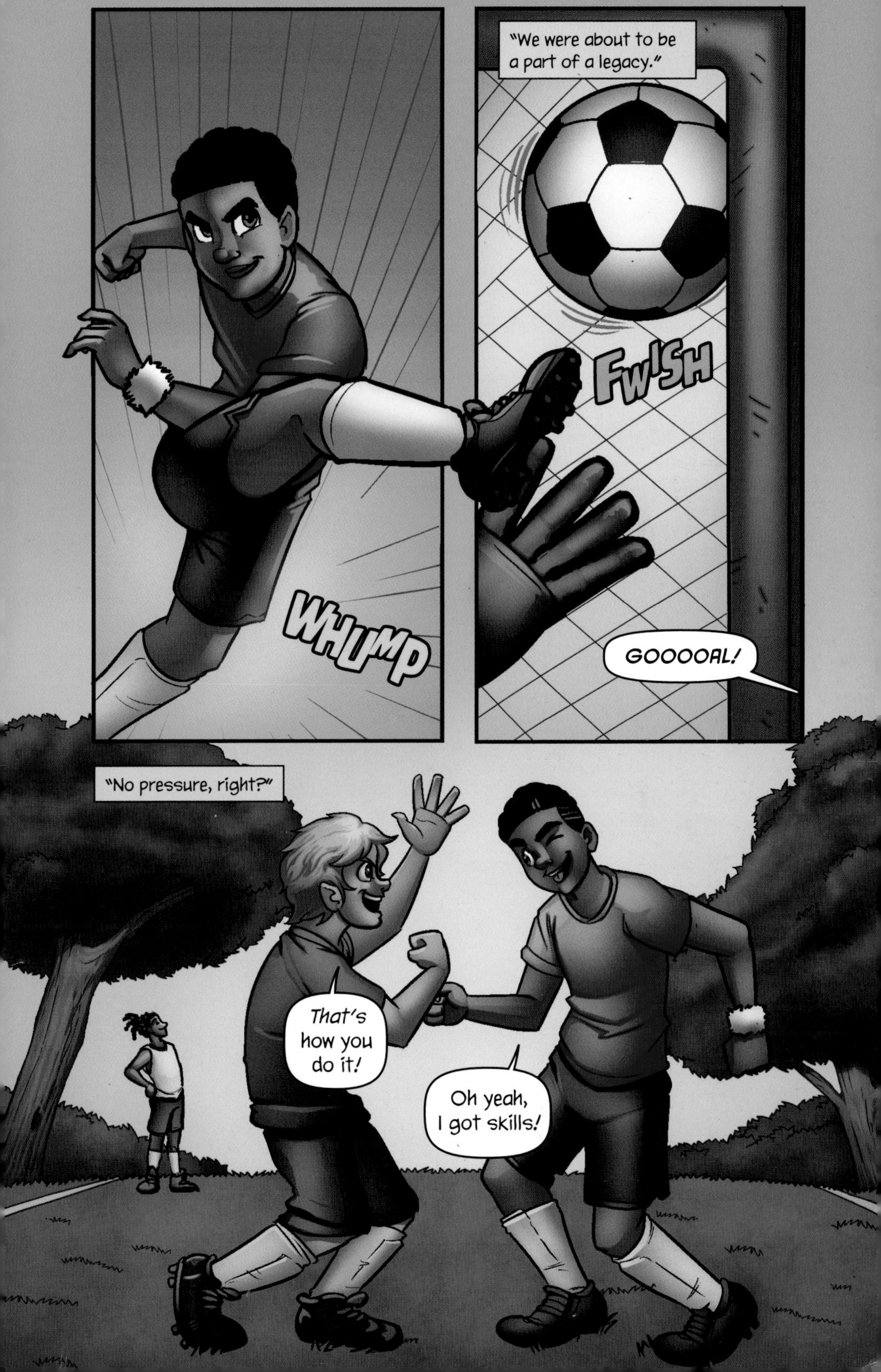
WHUMP
"We were about to be a part of a legacy."
FWISH
GOOOOAL!
"No pressure, right?"
That's how you do it!
Oh yeah, I got skills!

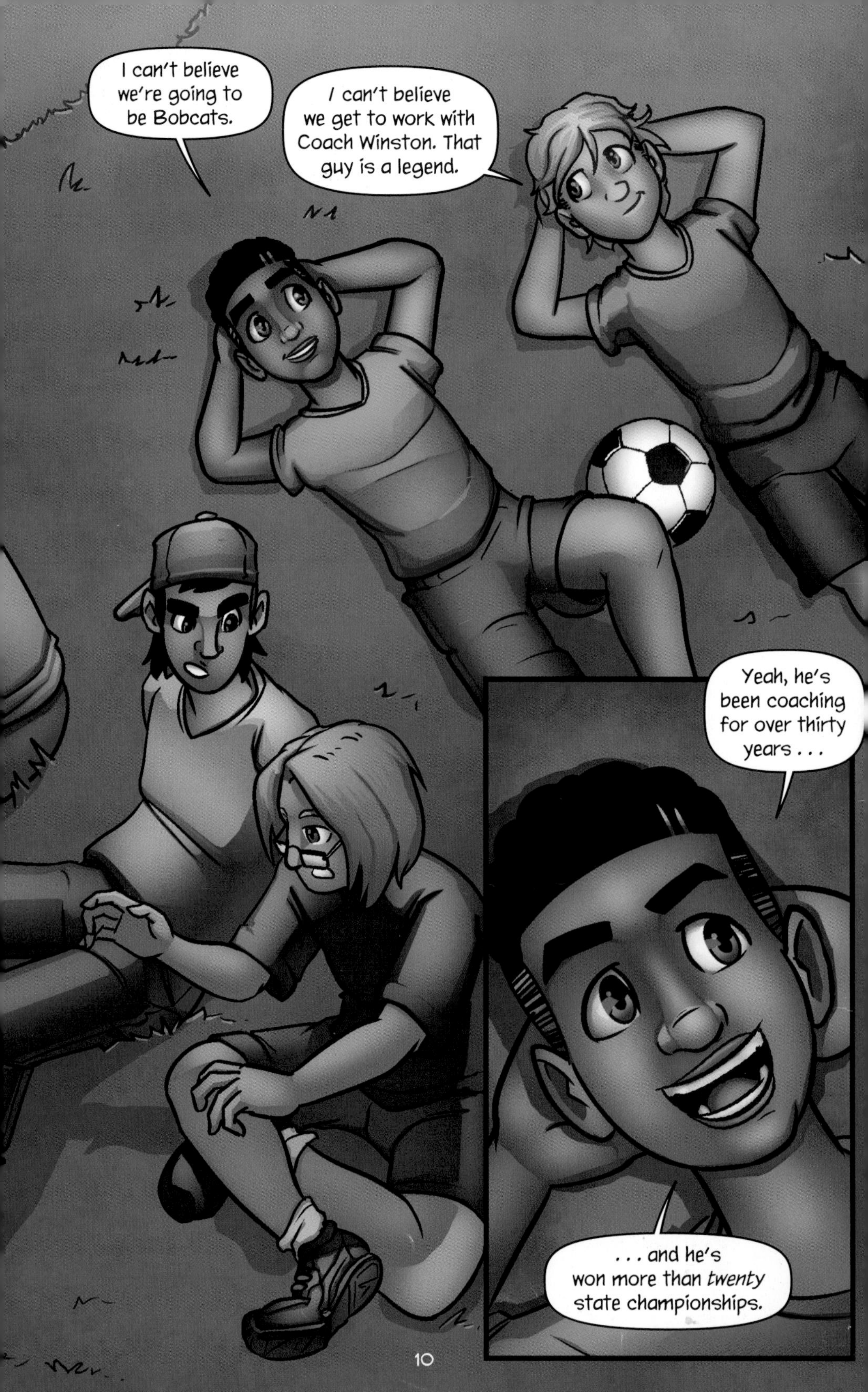
I can't believe we're going to be Bobcats.
I can't believe we get to work with Coach Winston. That guy is a legend.
Yeah, he's been coaching for over thirty years . . .
. . . and he's won more than *twenty* state championships.

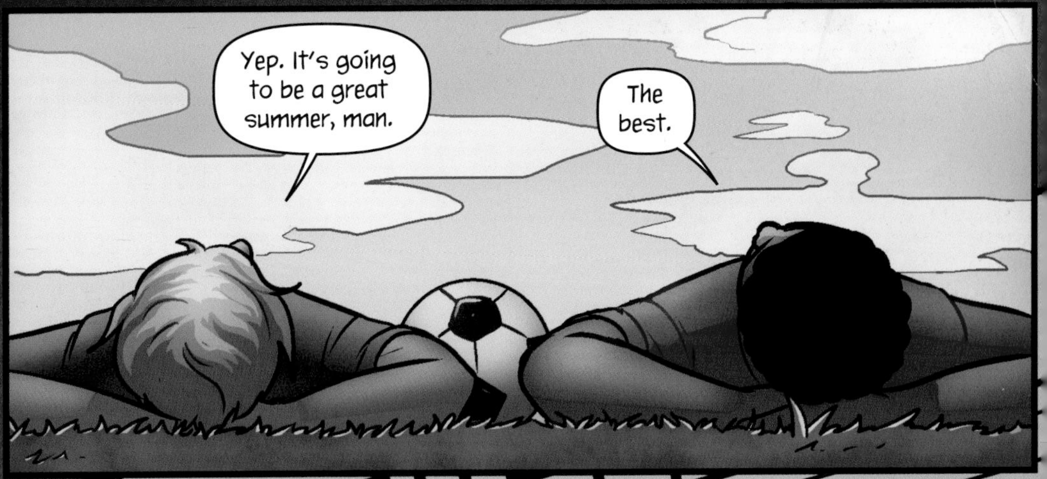
Yep. It's going to be a great summer, man.
The best.

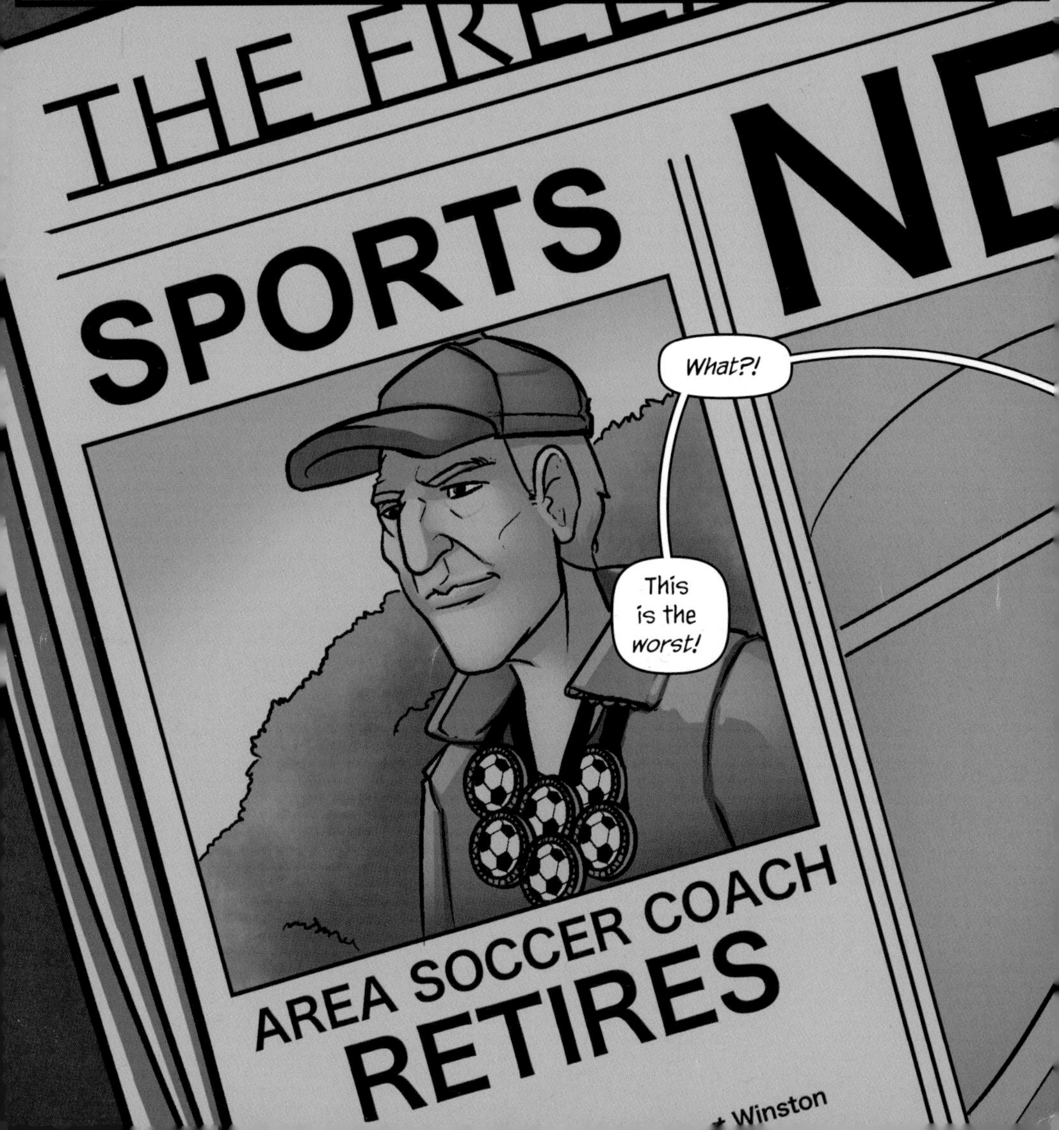
SPORTS
What?!
This is the *worst!*
AREA SOCCER COACH
RETIRES
Winston

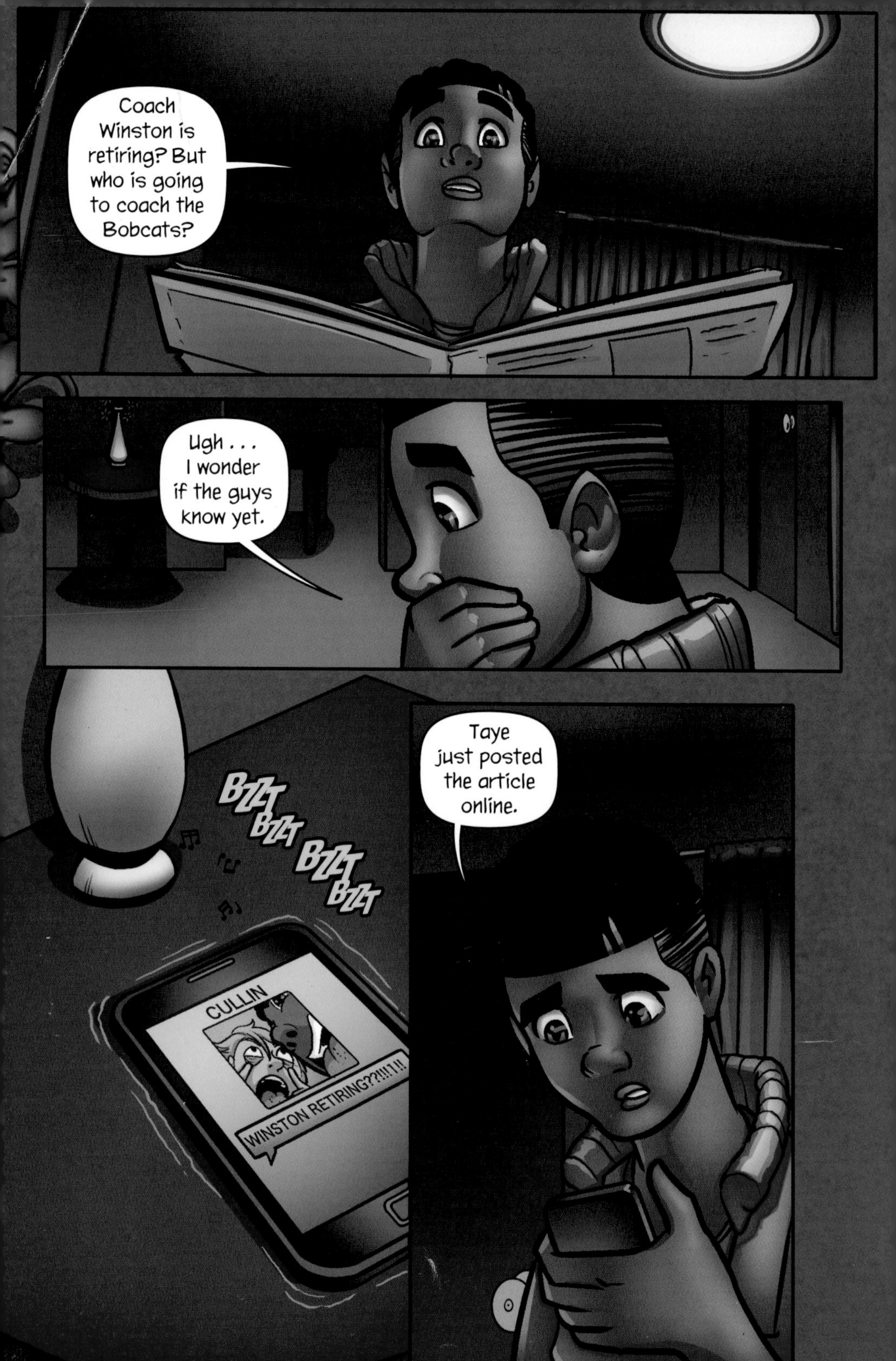
Coach Winston is retiring? But who is going to coach the Bobcats?
Ugh . . . I wonder if the guys know yet.
BZZT BZZT BZZT BZZT
CULLIN
WINSTON RETIRING??!!!1!!
Taye just posted the article online.

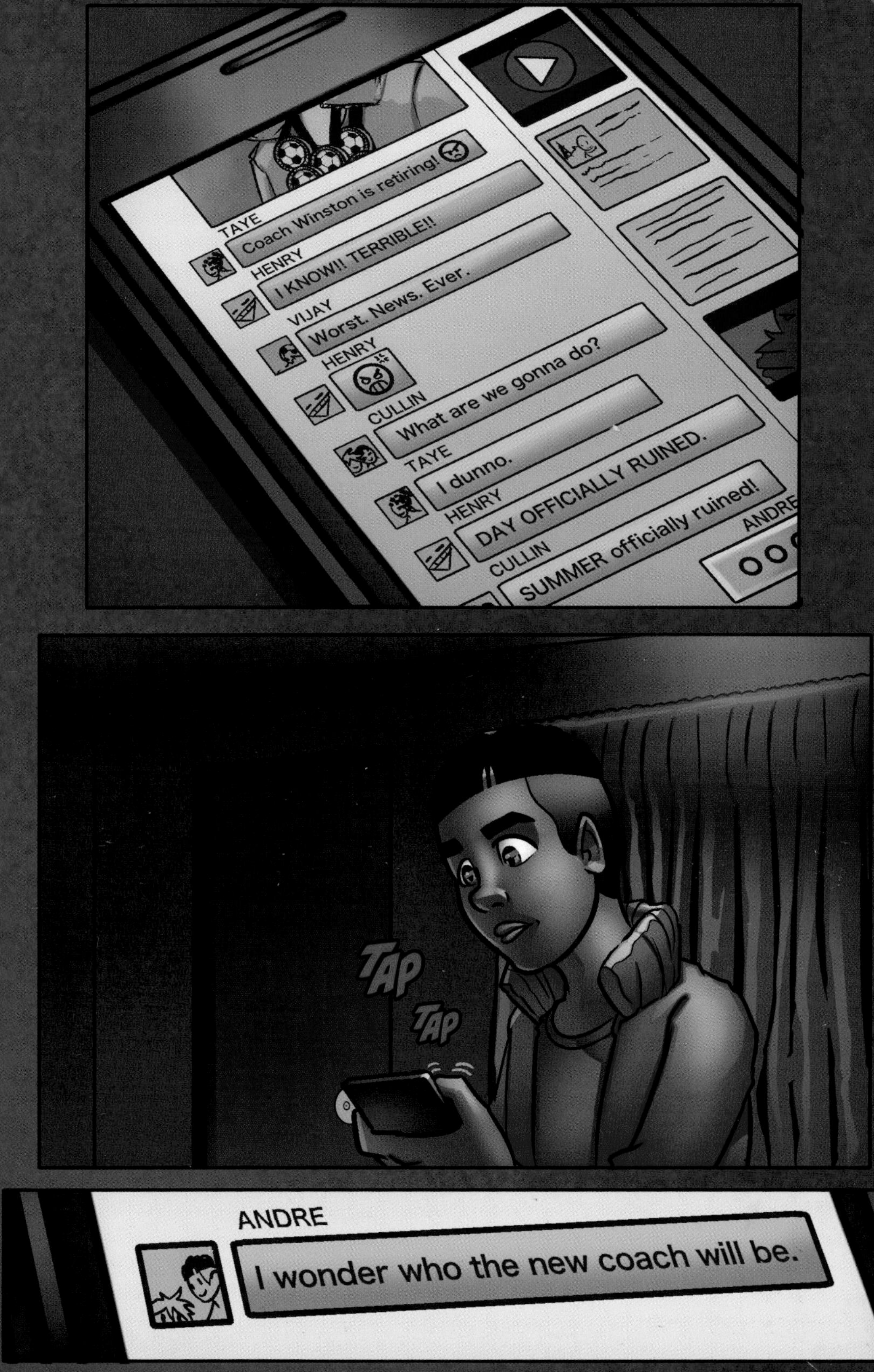
TAYE
Coach Winston is retiring!
HENRY
I KNOW!! TERRIBLE!!
VIJAY
Worst. News. Ever.
HENRY
CULLIN
What are we gonna do?
TAYE
I dunno.
HENRY
DAY OFFICIALLY RUINED.
CULLIN
SUMMER officially ruined!
TAP
TAP
ANDRE
I wonder who the new coach will be.

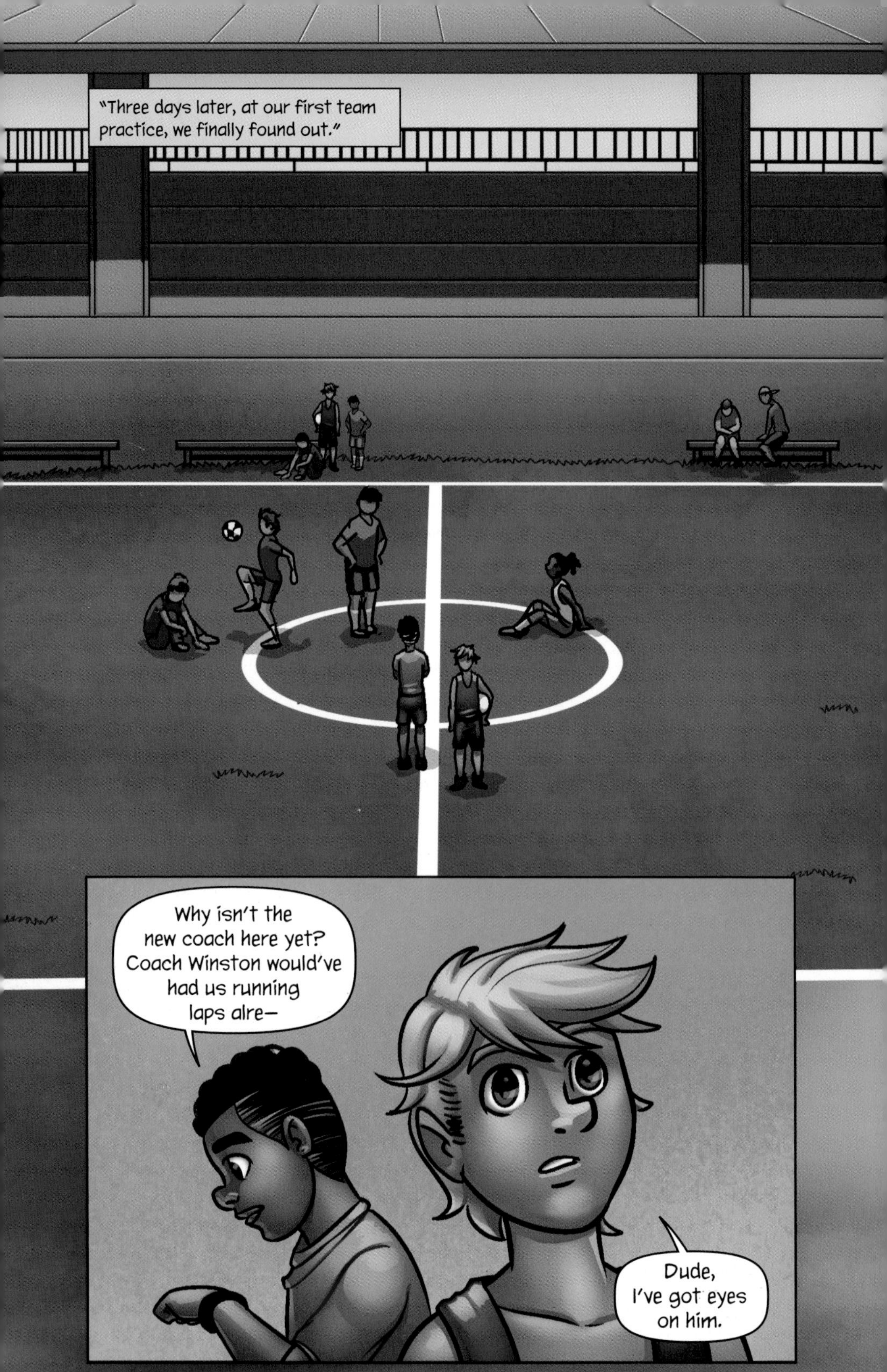
"Three days later, at our first team practice, we finally found out."
Why isn't the new coach here yet? Coach Winston would've had us running laps alre—
Dude, I've got eyes on him.

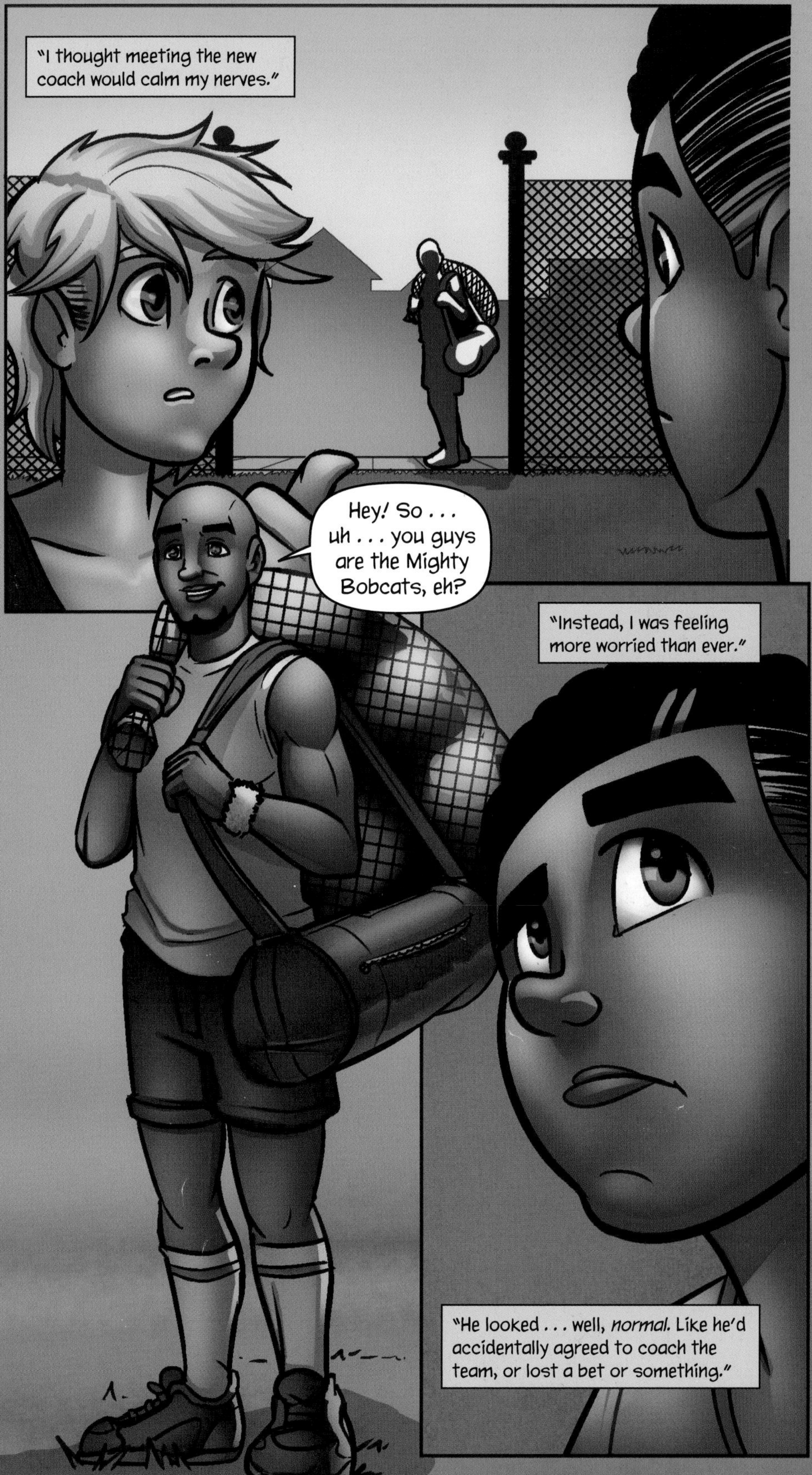
"I thought meeting the new coach would calm my nerves."
Hey! So . . . uh . . . you guys are the Mighty Bobcats, eh?
"Instead, I was feeling more worried than ever."
"He looked . . . well, *normal.* Like he'd accidentally agreed to coach the team, or lost a bet or something."

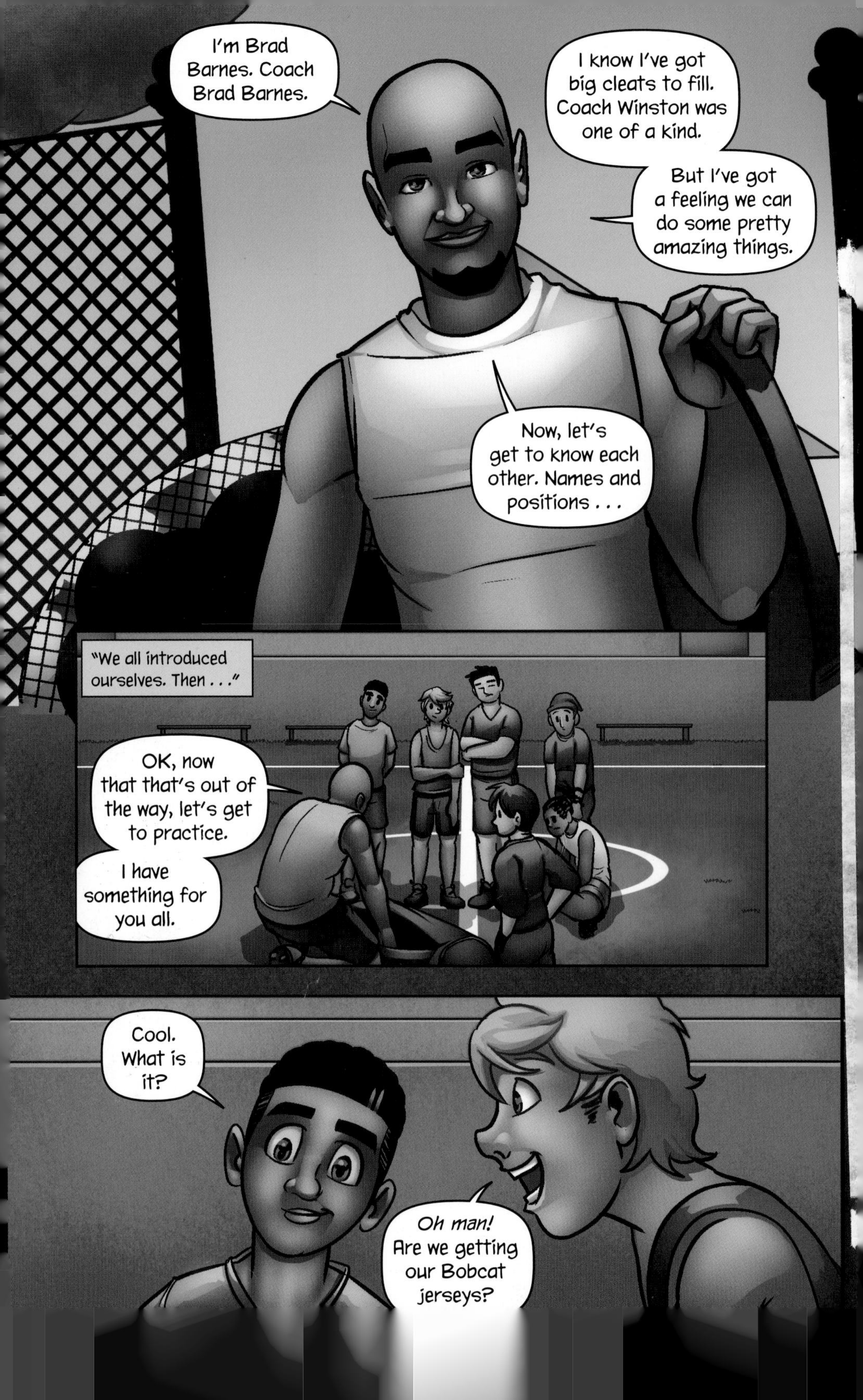
I'm Brad Barnes. Coach Brad Barnes.
I know I've got big cleats to fill. Coach Winston was one of a kind.
But I've got a feeling we can do some pretty amazing things.
Now, let's get to know each other. Names and positions . . .
"We all introduced ourselves. Then . . ."
OK, now that that's out of the way, let's get to practice.
I have something for you all.
Cool. What is it?
Oh man! Are we getting our Bobcat jerseys?

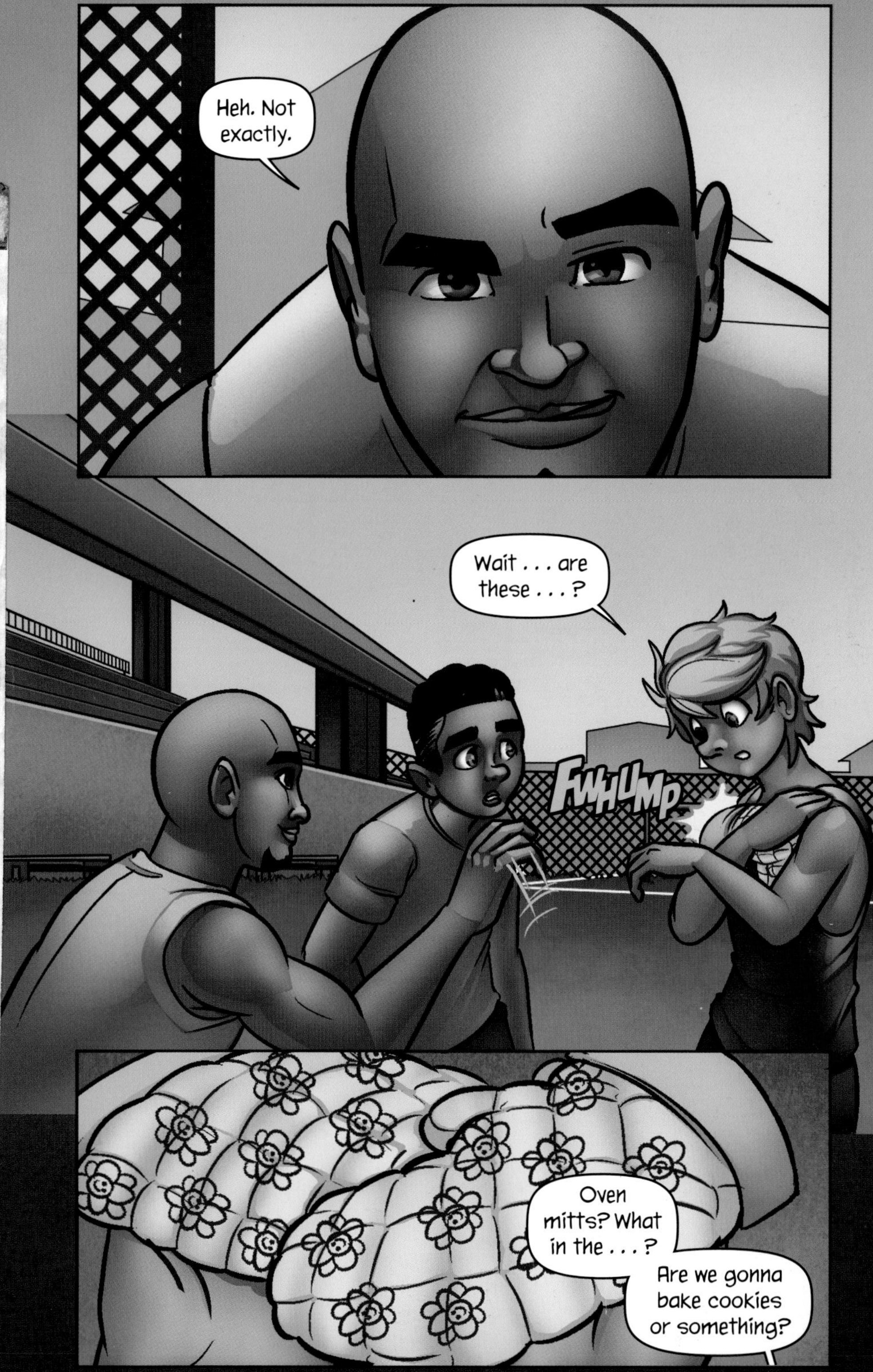
Heh. Not exactly.
Wait . . . are these . . . ?
FWHUMP
Oven mitts? What in the . . . ?
Are we gonna bake cookies or something?

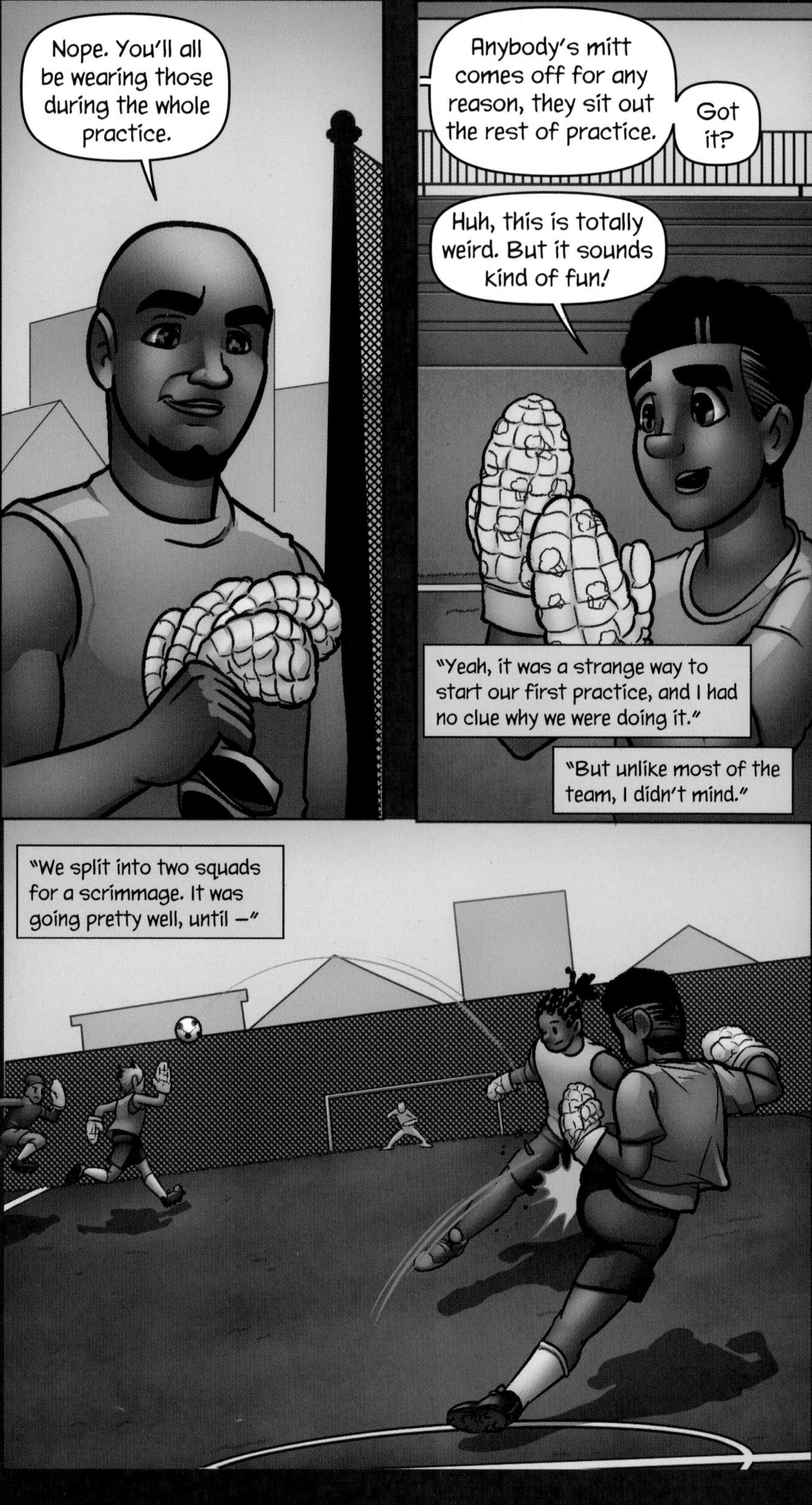
Nope. You'll all be wearing those during the whole practice.
Anybody's mitt comes off for any reason, they sit out the rest of practice.
Got it?
Huh, this is totally weird. But it sounds kind of fun!
"Yeah, it was a strange way to start our first practice, and I had no clue why we were doing it."
"But unlike most of the team, I didn't mind."
"We split into two squads for a scrimmage. It was going pretty well, until —"

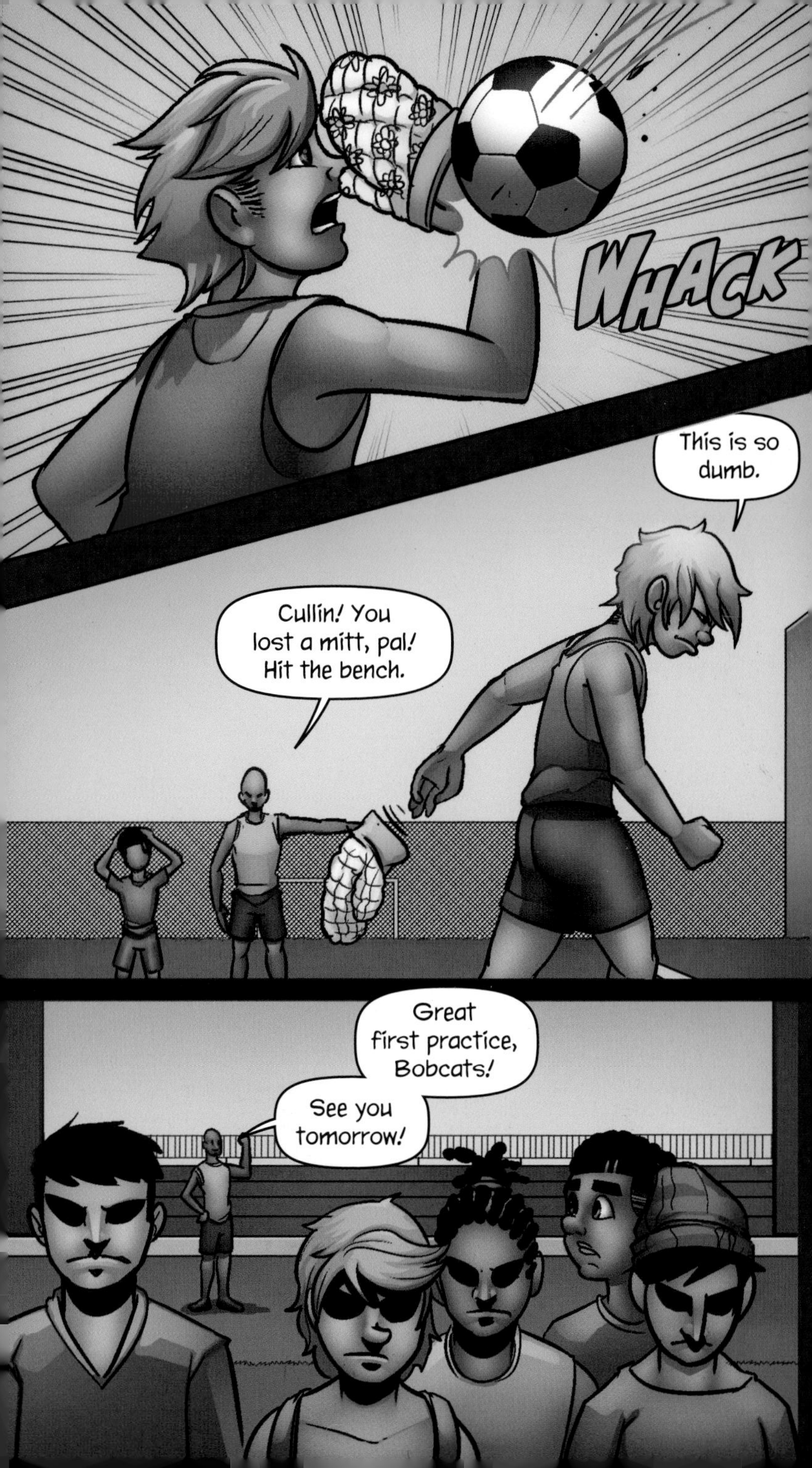
WHACK
This is so dumb.
Cullin! You lost a mitt, pal! Hit the bench.
Great first practice, Bobcats!
See you tomorrow!

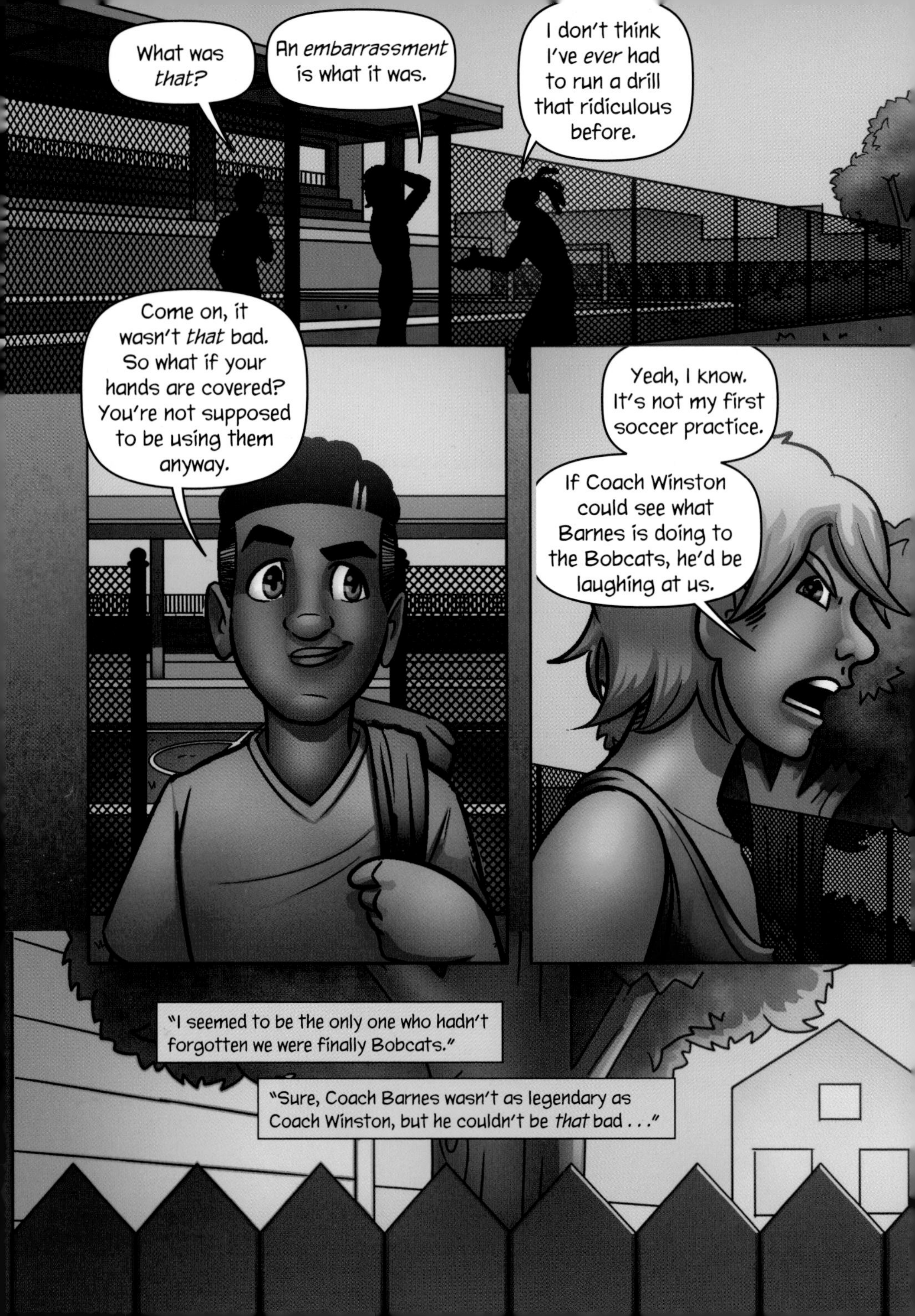
What was *that*?
An *embarrassment* is what it was.
I don't think I've *ever* had to run a drill that ridiculous before.
Come on, it wasn't *that* bad. So what if your hands are covered? You're not supposed to be using them anyway.
Yeah, I know. It's not my first soccer practice.
If Coach Winston could see what Barnes is doing to the Bobcats, he'd be laughing at us.
"I seemed to be the only one who hadn't forgotten we were finally Bobcats."
"Sure, Coach Barnes wasn't as legendary as Coach Winston, but he couldn't be *that* bad . . ."

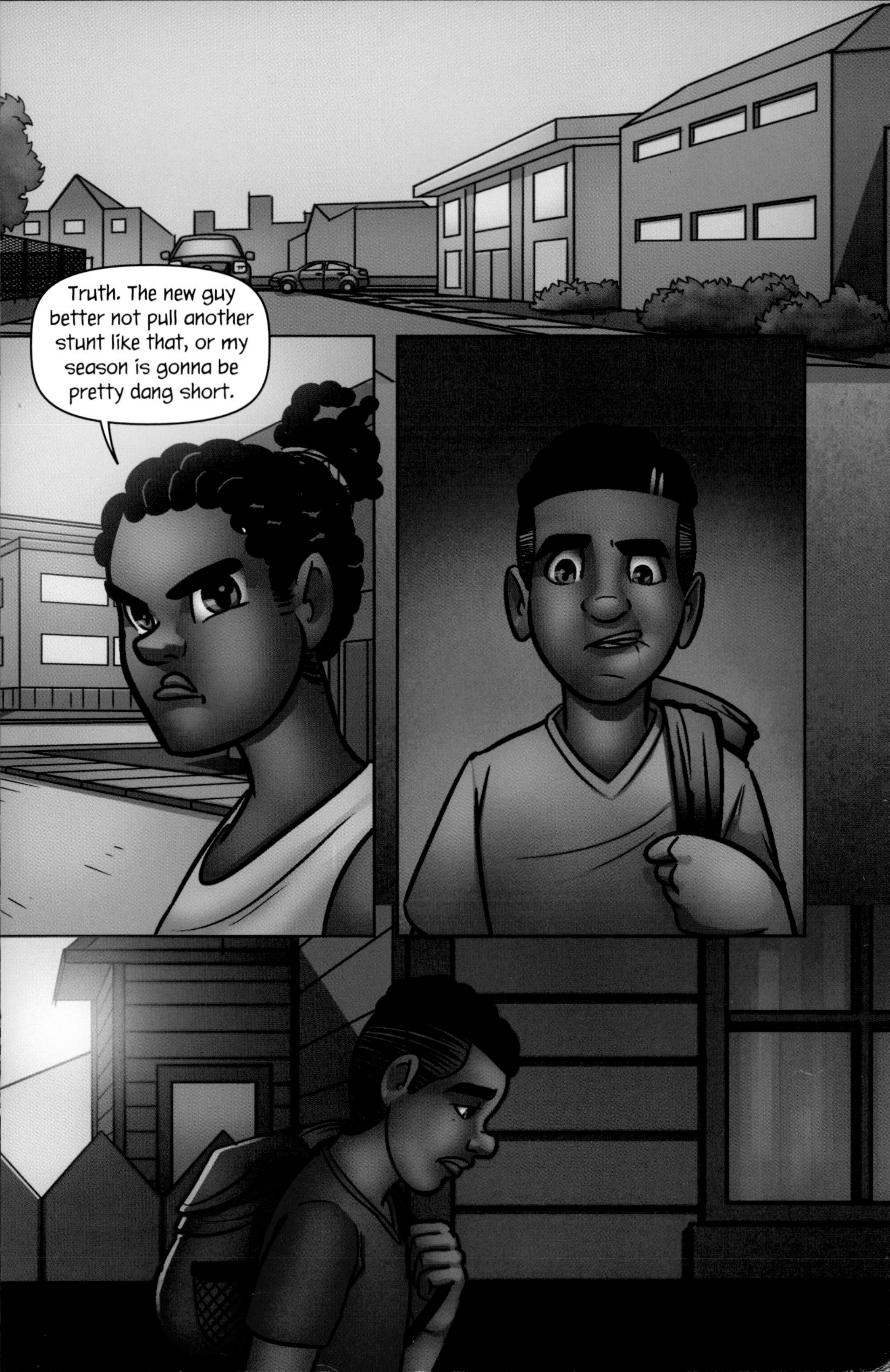
Truth. The new guy better not pull another stunt like that, or my season is gonna be pretty dang short.

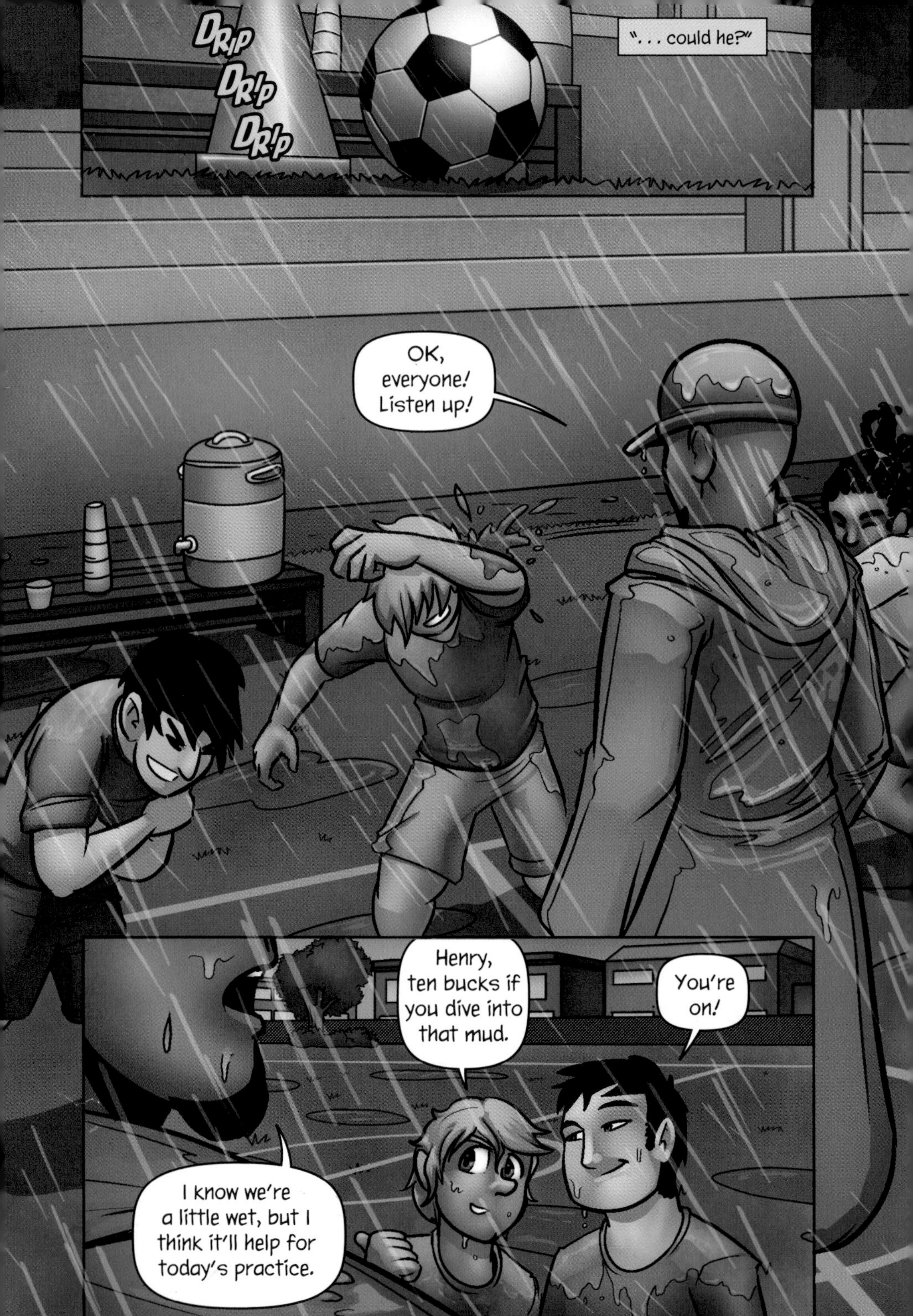
DRIP
DRIP
DRIP
". . . could he?"
OK, everyone! Listen up!
I know we're a little wet, but I think it'll help for today's practice.
Henry, ten bucks if you dive into that mud.
You're on!

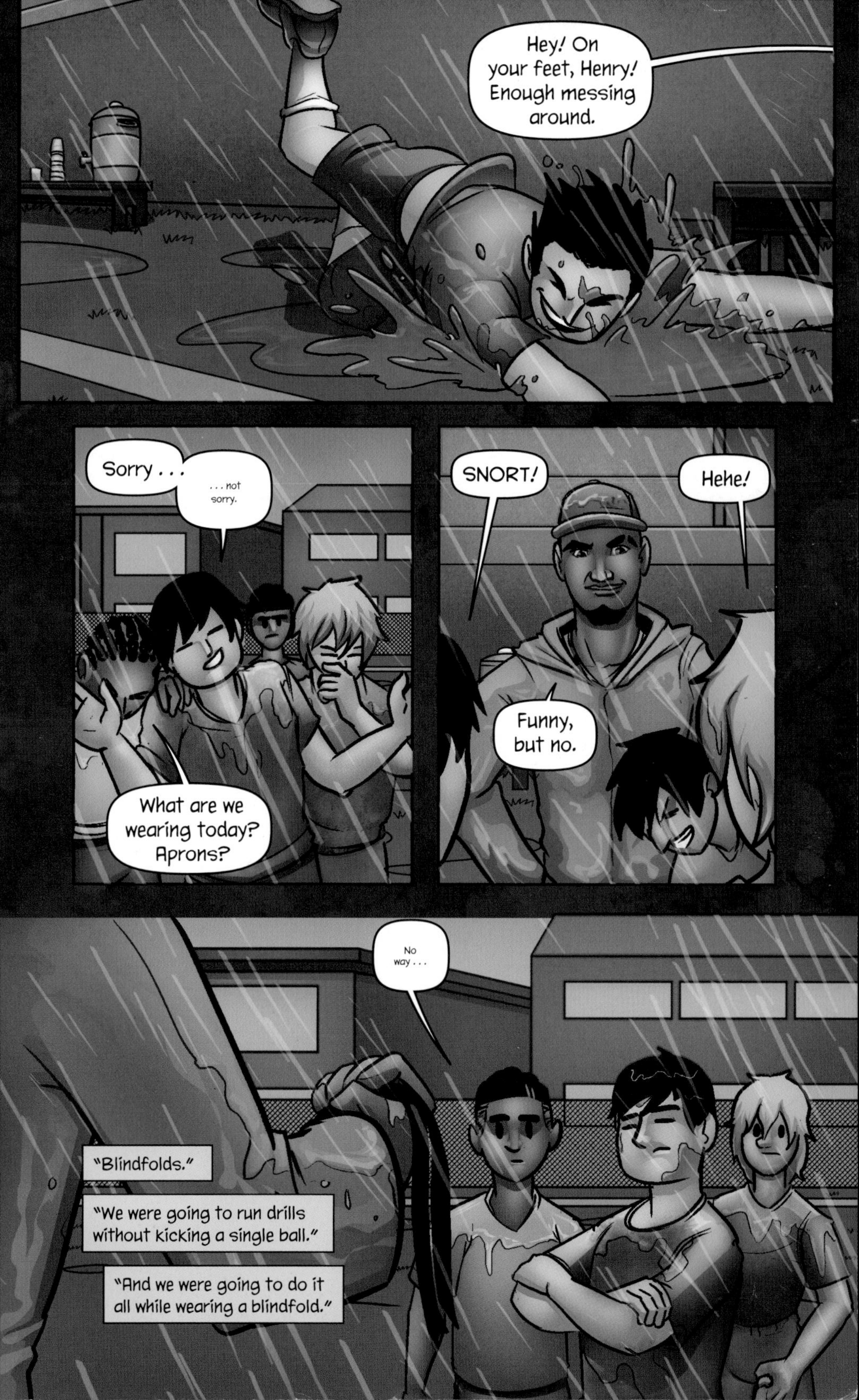
Hey! On your feet, Henry! Enough messing around.
Sorry . . .
. . . not sorry.
What are we wearing today? Aprons?
SNORT!
Hehe!
Funny, but no.
No way . . .
"Blindfolds."
"We were going to run drills without kicking a single ball."
"And we were going to do it all while wearing a blindfold."

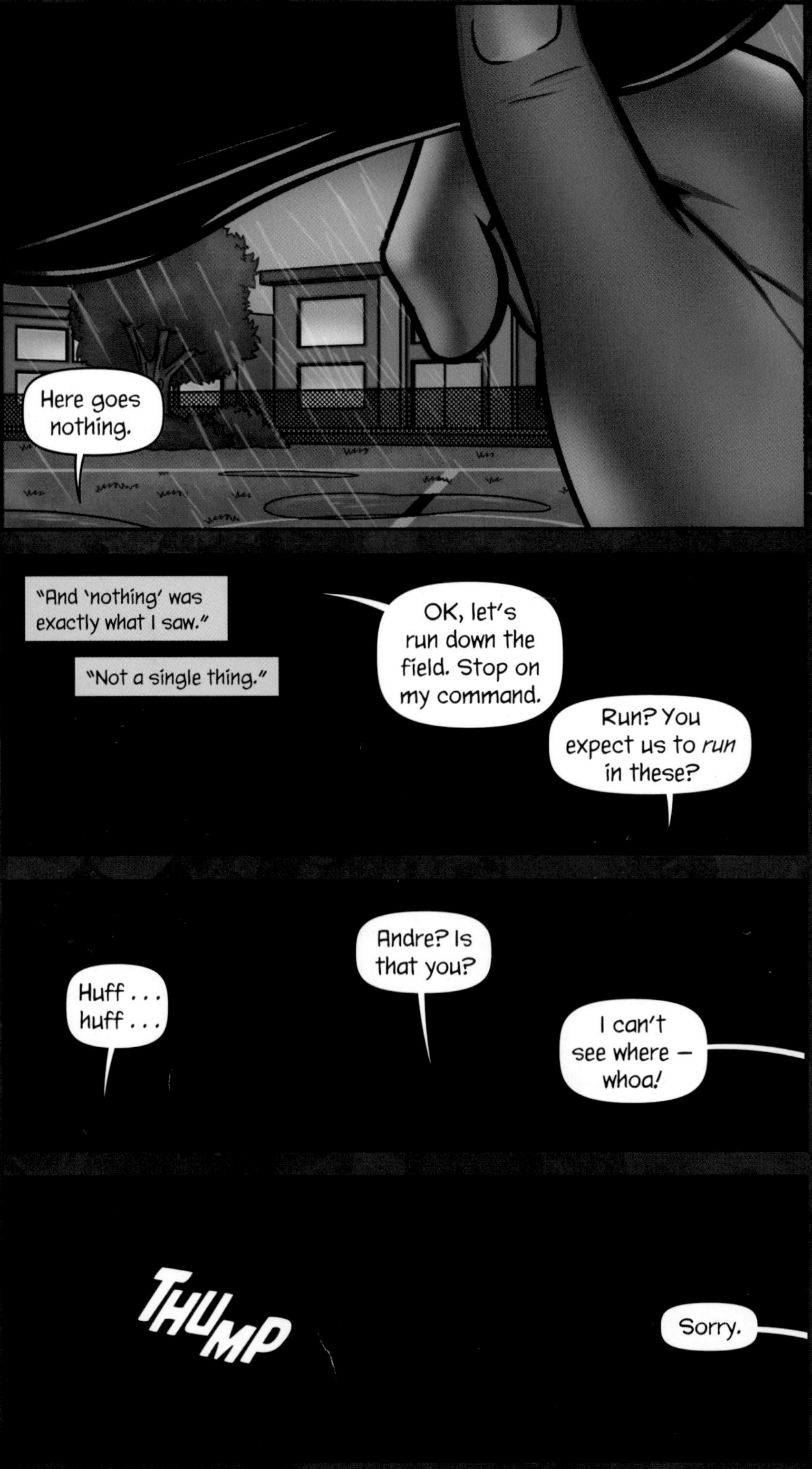
Here goes nothing.
"And 'nothing' was exactly what I saw."
"Not a single thing."
OK, let's run down the field. Stop on my command.
Run? You expect us to *run* in these?
Huff . . . huff . . .
Andre? Is that you?
I can't see where — whoa!
THUMP
Sorry.

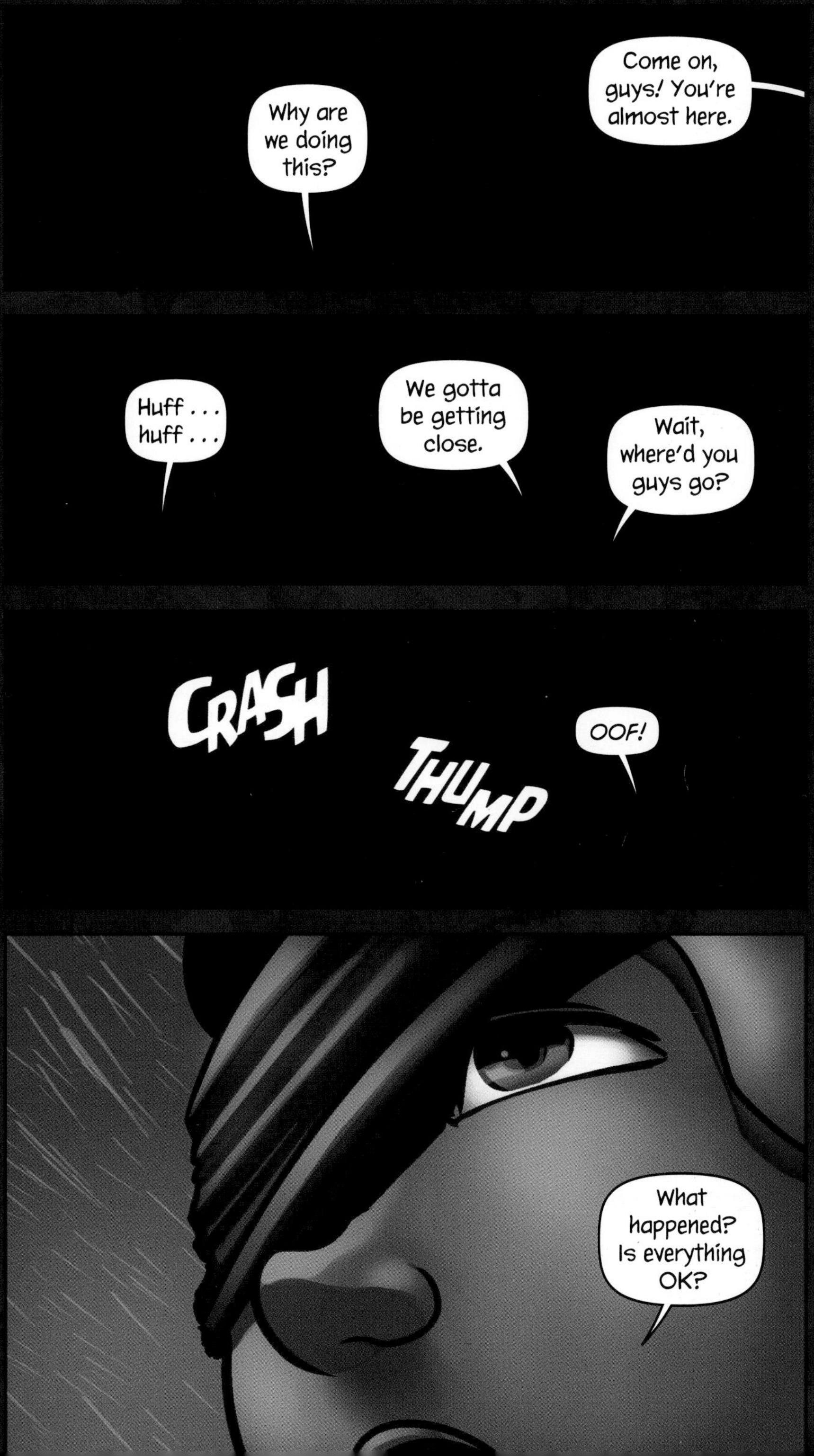
Why are we doing this?
Come on, guys! You're almost here.
Huff . . . huff . . .
We gotta be getting close.
Wait, where'd you guys go?
CRASH
THUMP
OOF!
What happened? Is everything OK?

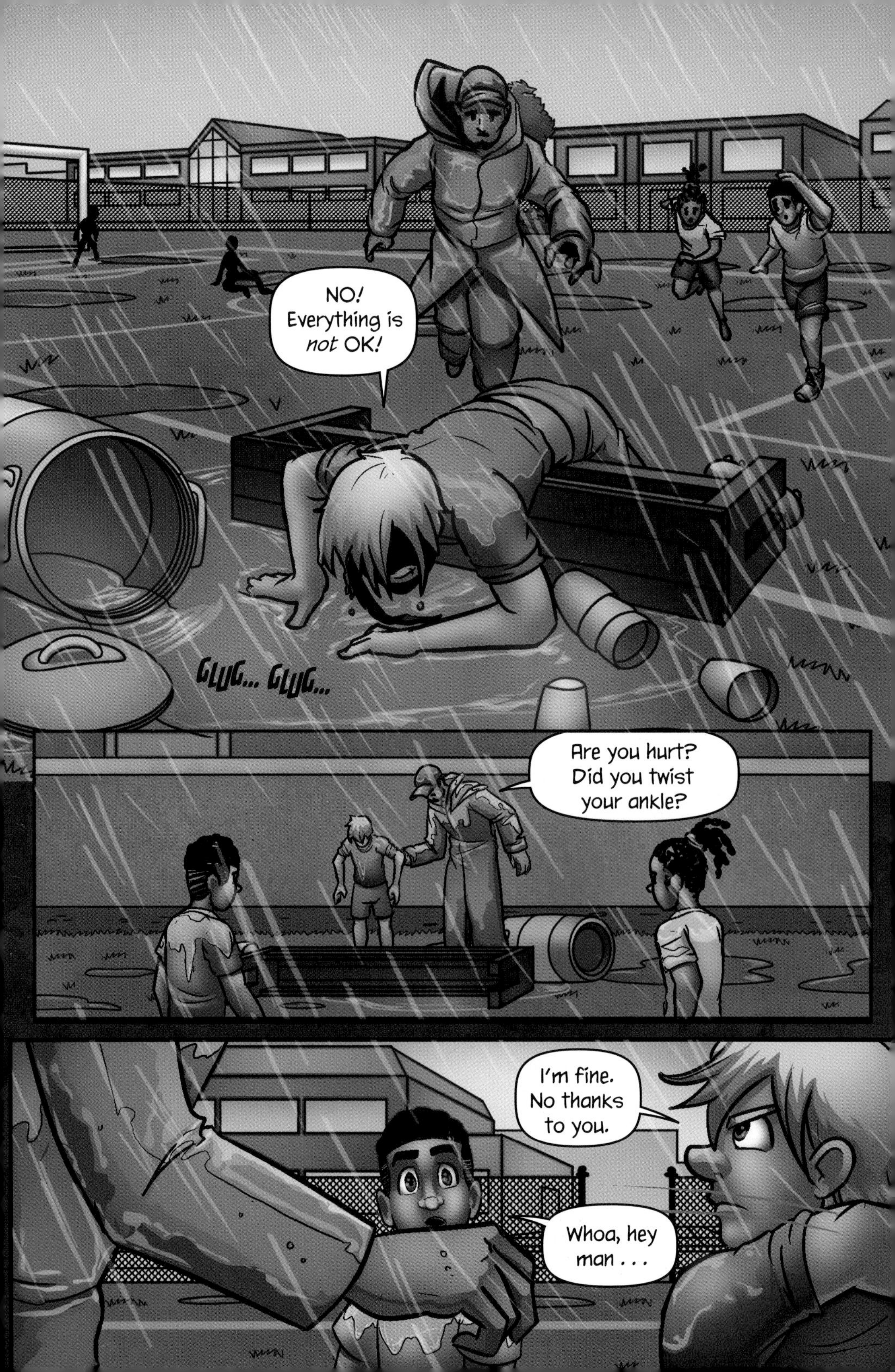
NO! Everything is *not* OK!
GLUG... GLUG...
Are you hurt? Did you twist your ankle?
I'm fine. No thanks to you.
Whoa, hey man . . .

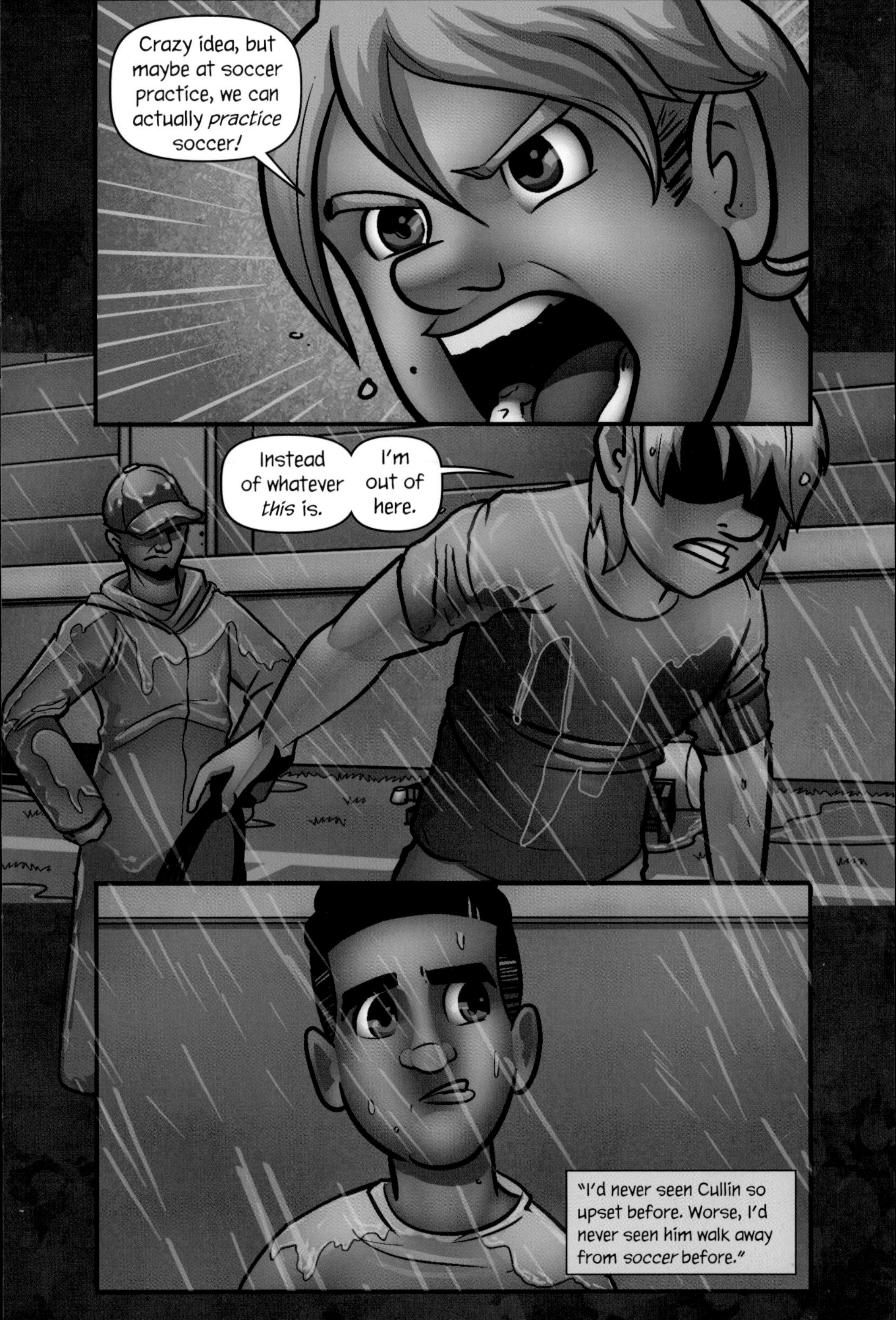
Crazy idea, but maybe at soccer practice, we can actually *practice* soccer!
Instead of whatever *this* is.
I'm out of here.
"I'd never seen Cullin so upset before. Worse, I'd never seen him walk away from *soccer* before."

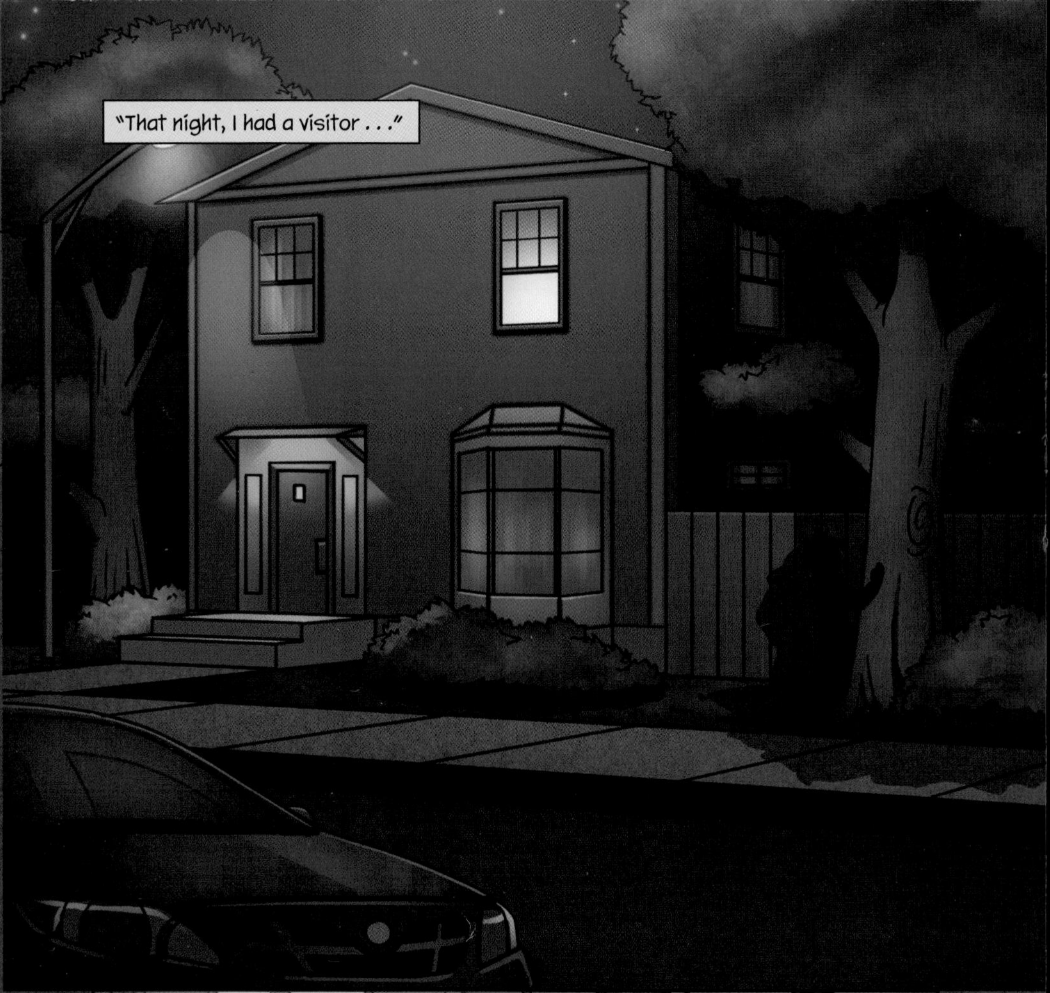
"That night, I had a visitor . . ."

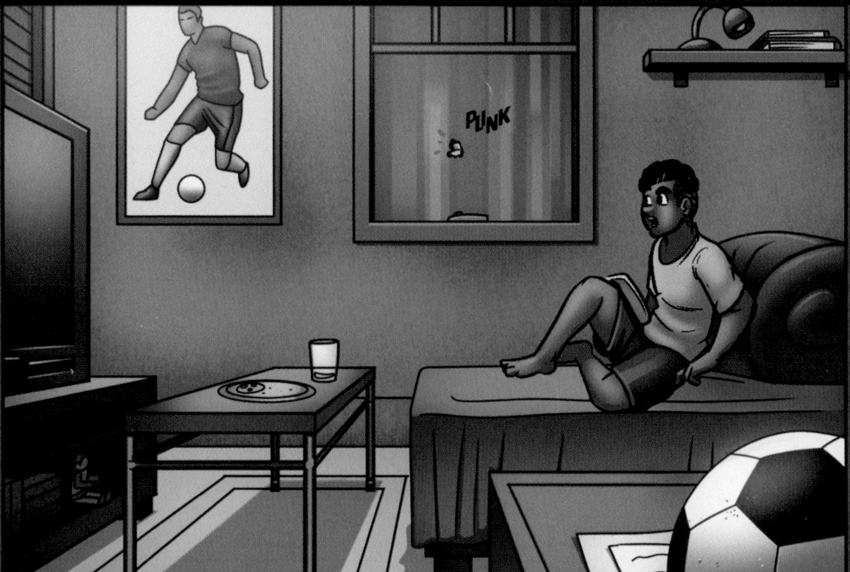
PLINK

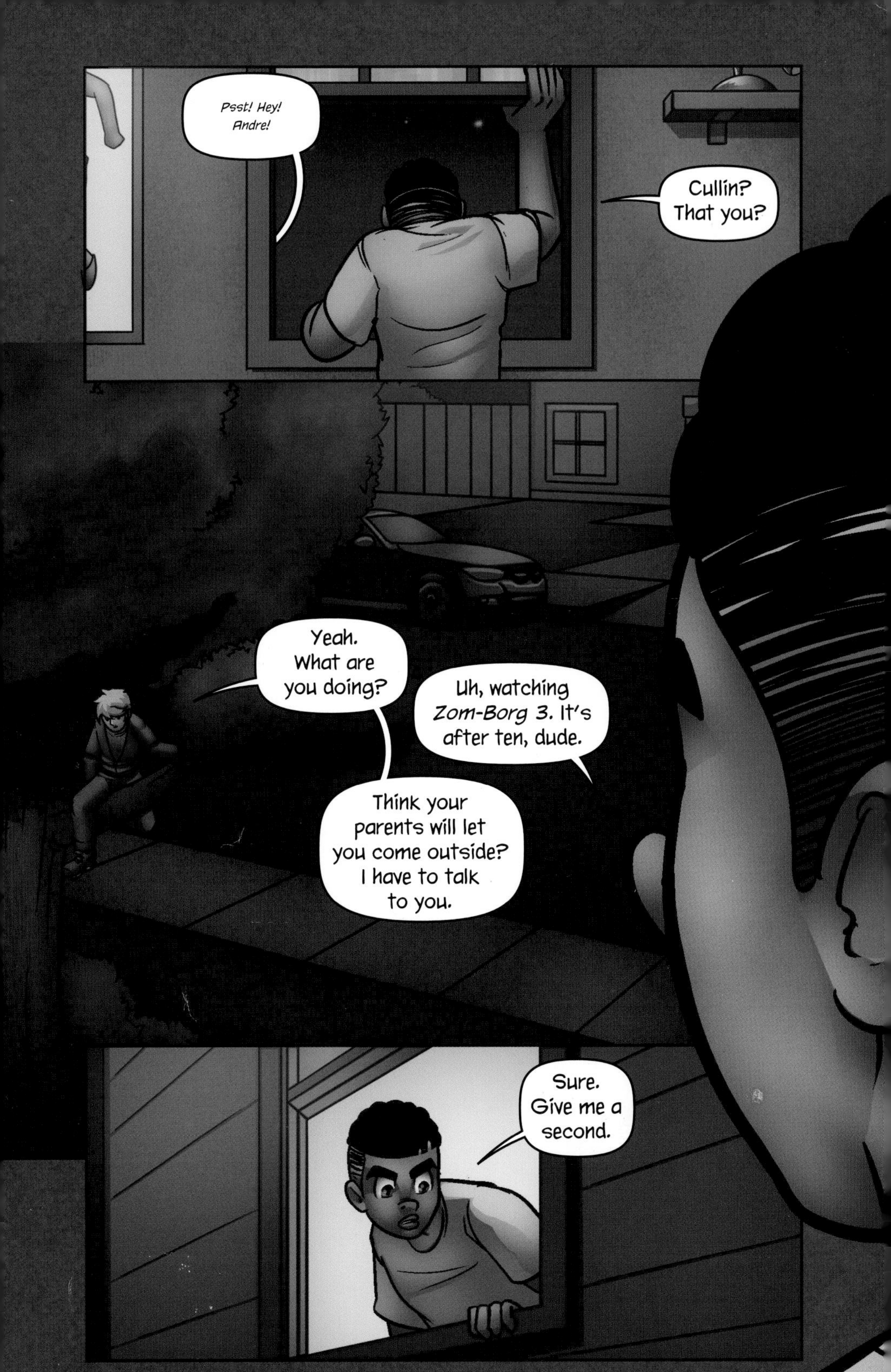
Psst! Hey! Andre!
Cullin? That you?
Yeah. What are you doing?
Uh, watching *Zom-Borg 3*. It's after ten, dude.
Think your parents will let you come outside? I have to talk to you.
Sure. Give me a second.

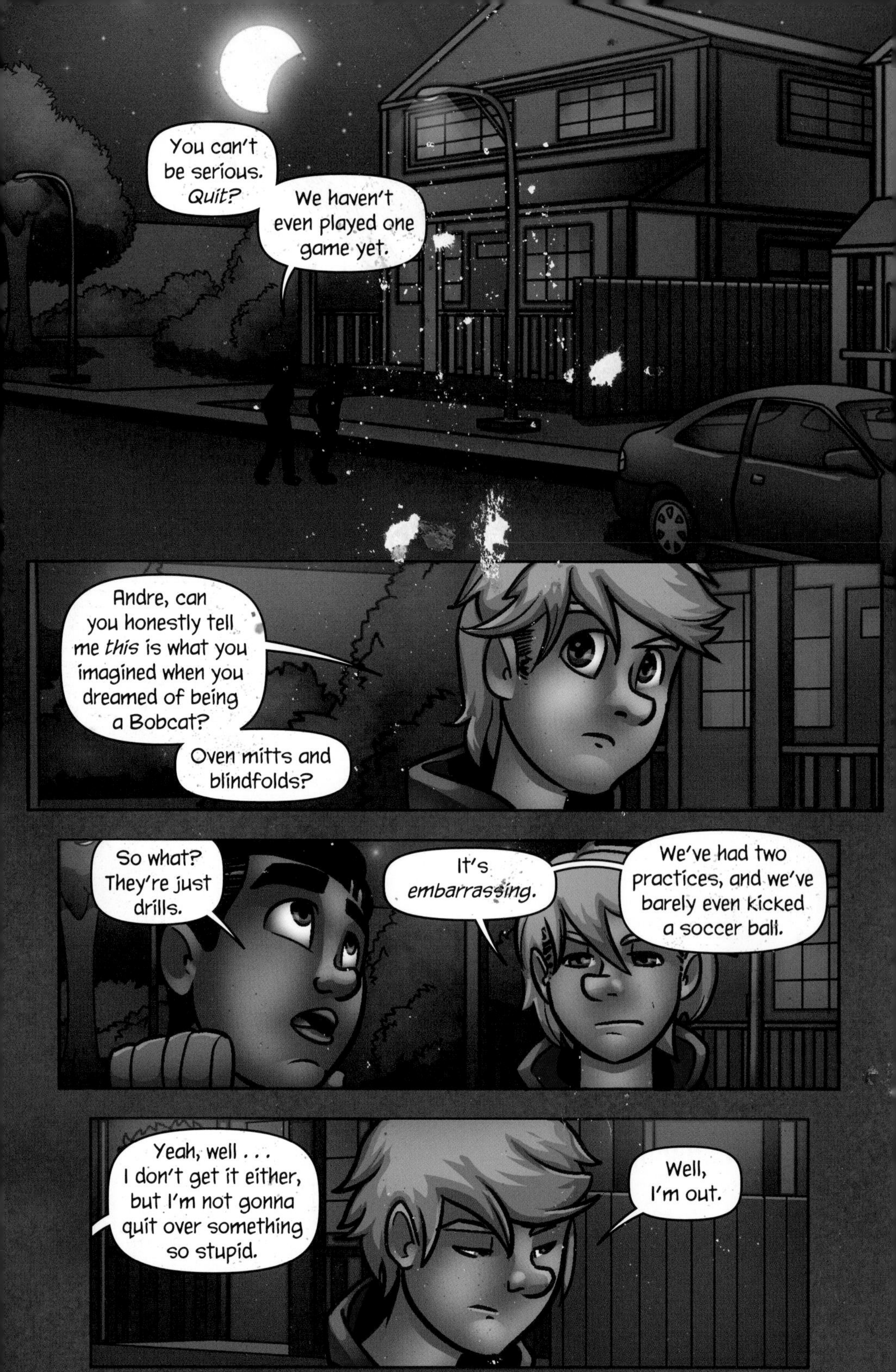
You can't be serious. *Quit?*
We haven't even played one game yet.
Andre, can you honestly tell me *this* is what you imagined when you dreamed of being a Bobcat?
Oven mitts and blindfolds?
So what? They're just drills.
It's *embarrassing*.
We've had two practices, and we've barely even kicked a soccer ball.
Yeah, well . . . I don't get it either, but I'm not gonna quit over something so stupid.
Well, I'm out.

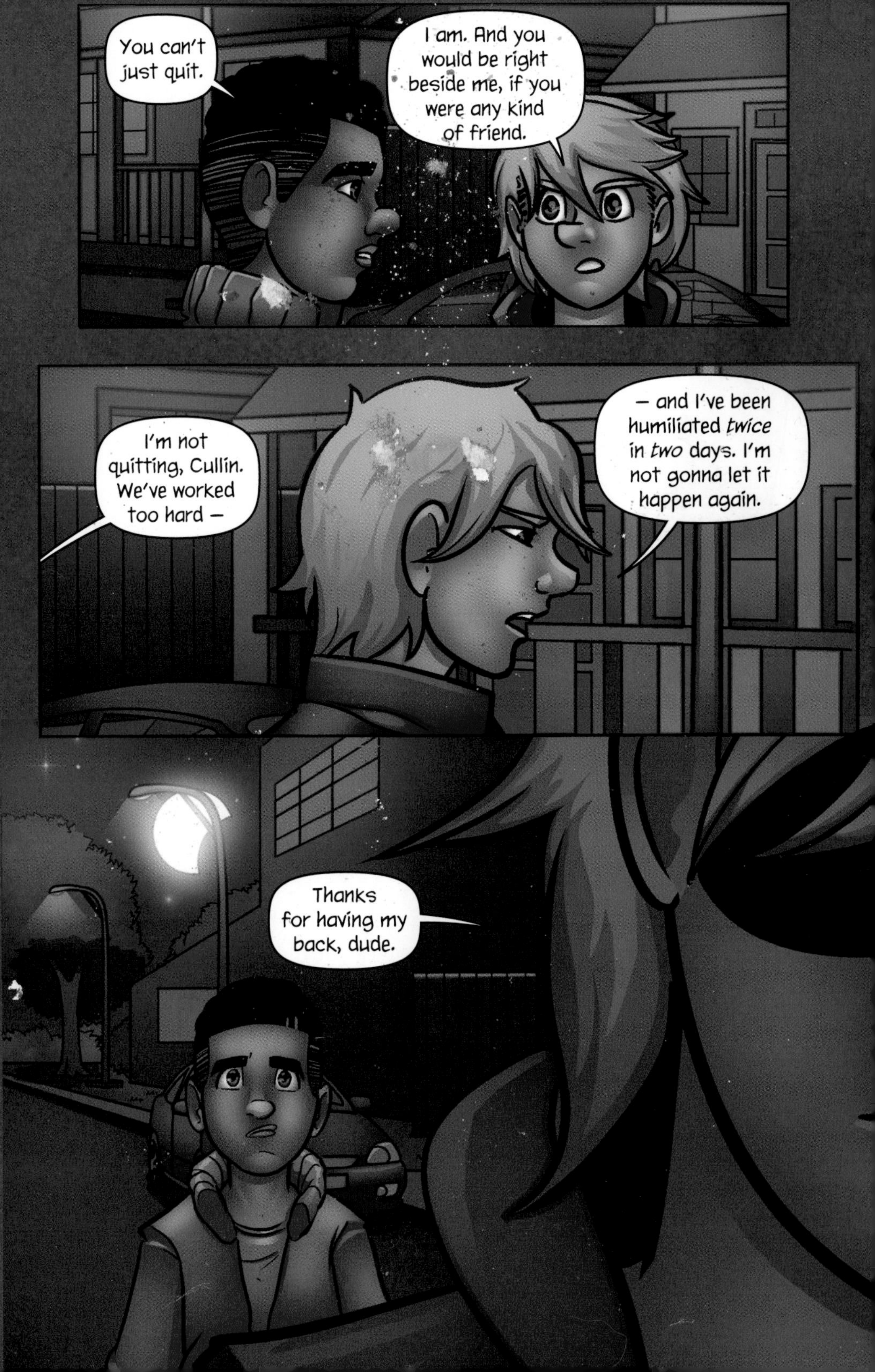
You can't just quit.
I am. And you would be right beside me, if you were any kind of friend.
I'm not quitting, Cullin. We've worked too hard —
— and I've been humiliated *twice* in *two* days. I'm not gonna let it happen again.
Thanks for having my back, dude.

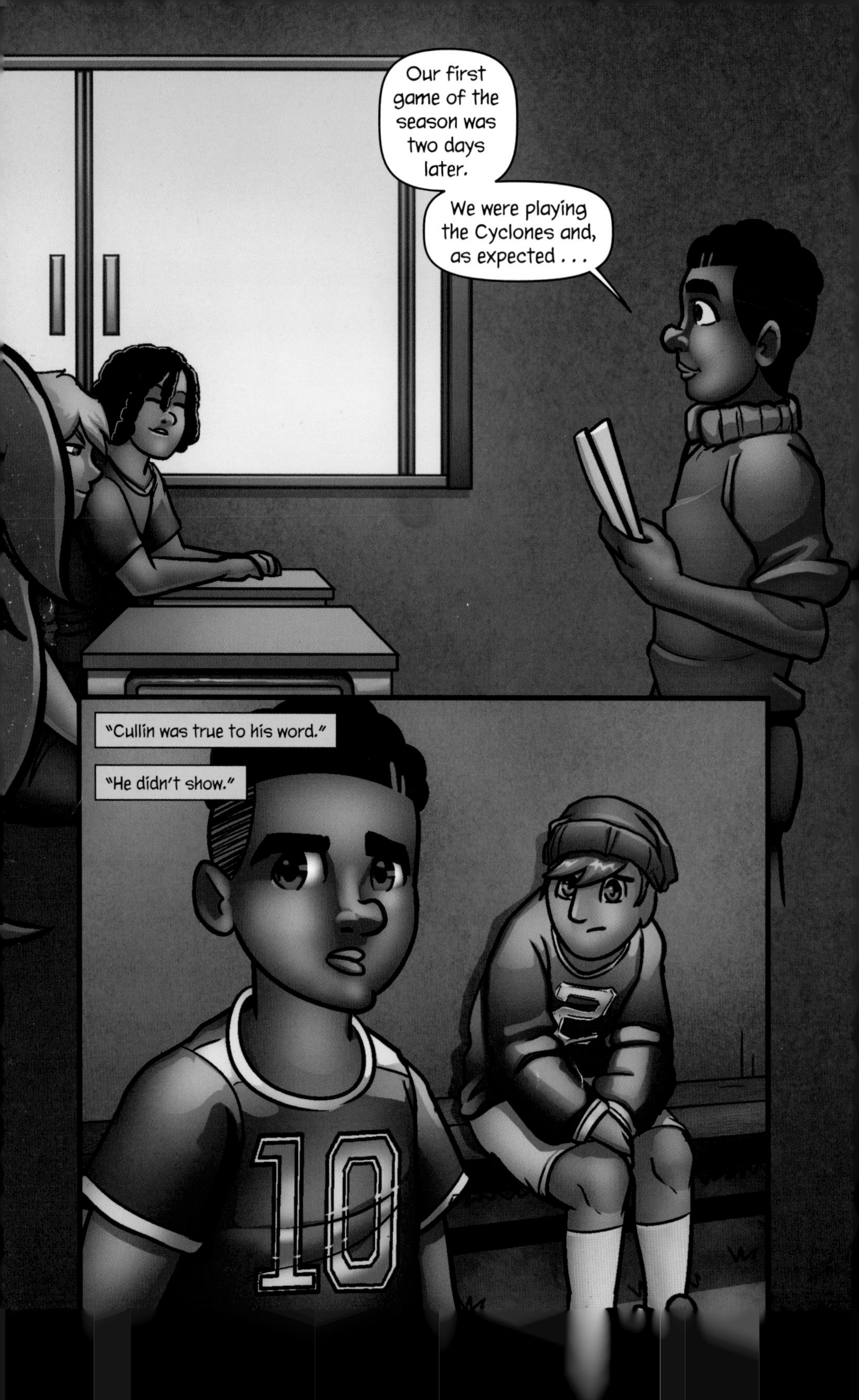
Our first game of the season was two days later.
We were playing the Cyclones and, as expected . . .
"Cullin was true to his word."
"He didn't show."

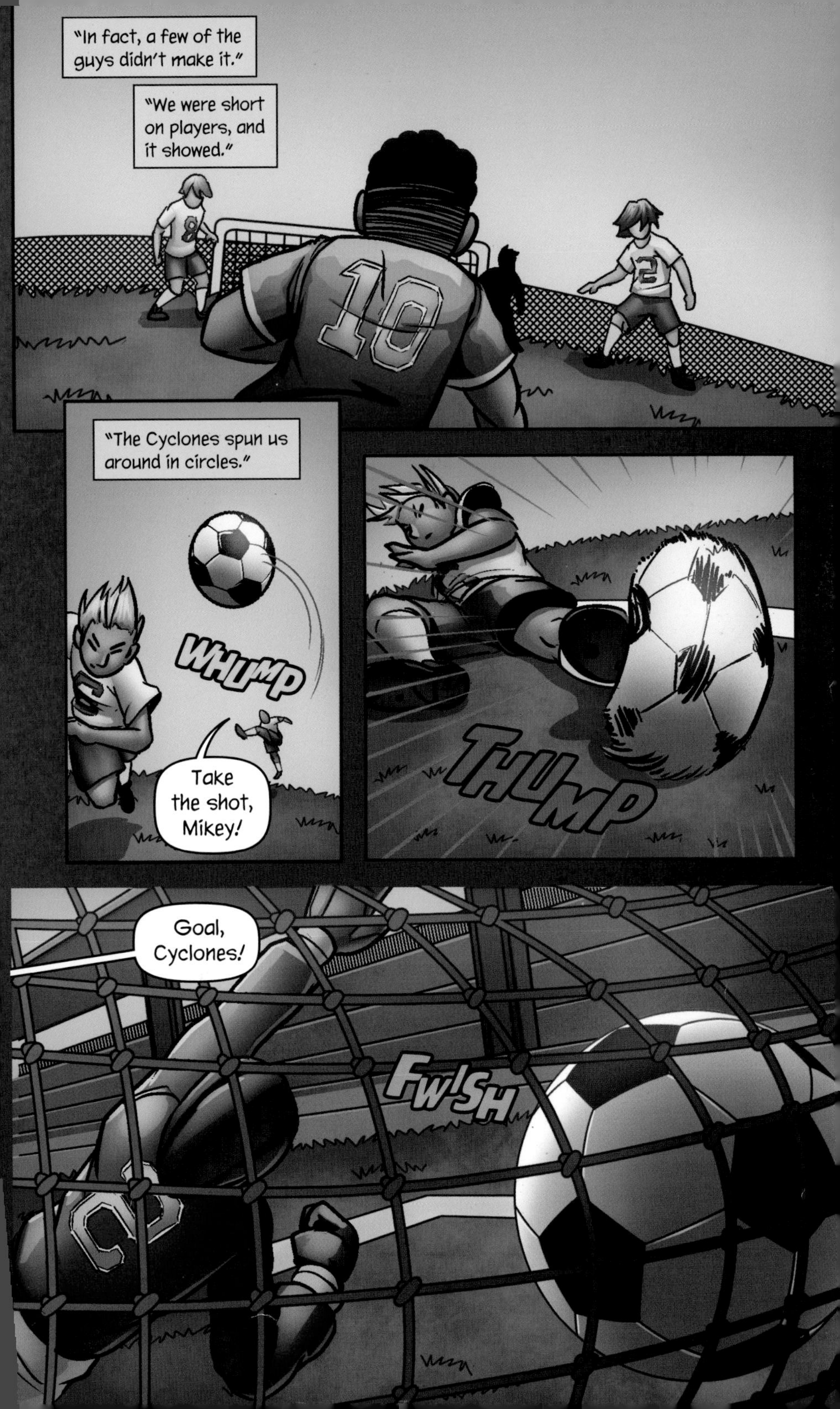
"In fact, a few of the guys didn't make it."
"We were short on players, and it showed."
"The Cyclones spun us around in circles."
WHUMP
Take the shot, Mikey!
THUMP
Goal, Cyclones!
FWISH

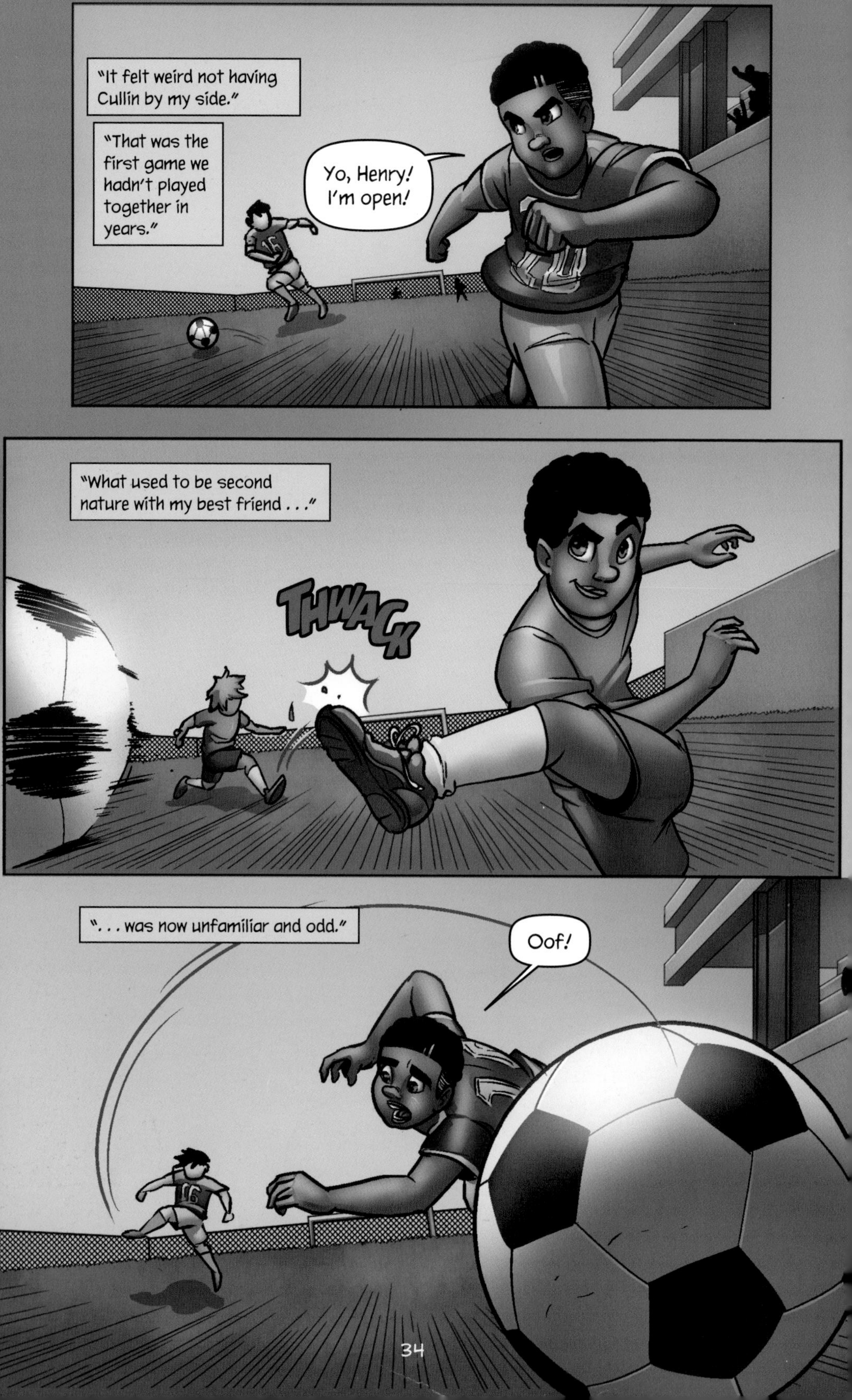
"It felt weird not having Cullin by my side."
"That was the first game we hadn't played together in years."
Yo, Henry! I'm open!
"What used to be second nature with my best friend . . ."
THWACK
". . . was now unfamiliar and odd."
Oof!

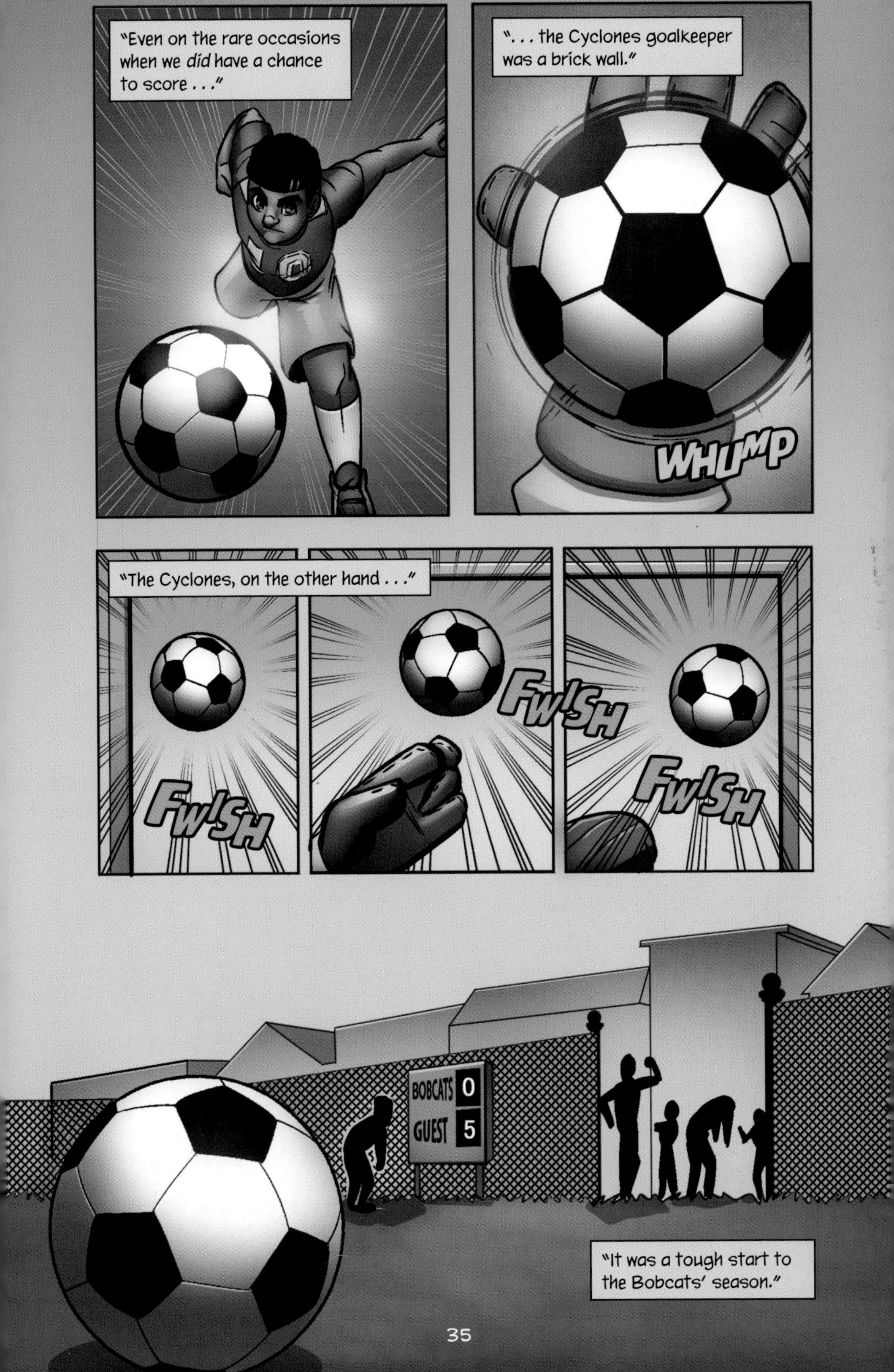
"Even on the rare occasions when we *did* have a chance to score . . ."
". . . the Cyclones goalkeeper was a brick wall."
WHUMP
"The Cyclones, on the other hand . . ."
FWISH
FWISH
FWISH
BOBCATS 0
GUEST 5
"It was a tough start to the Bobcats' season."

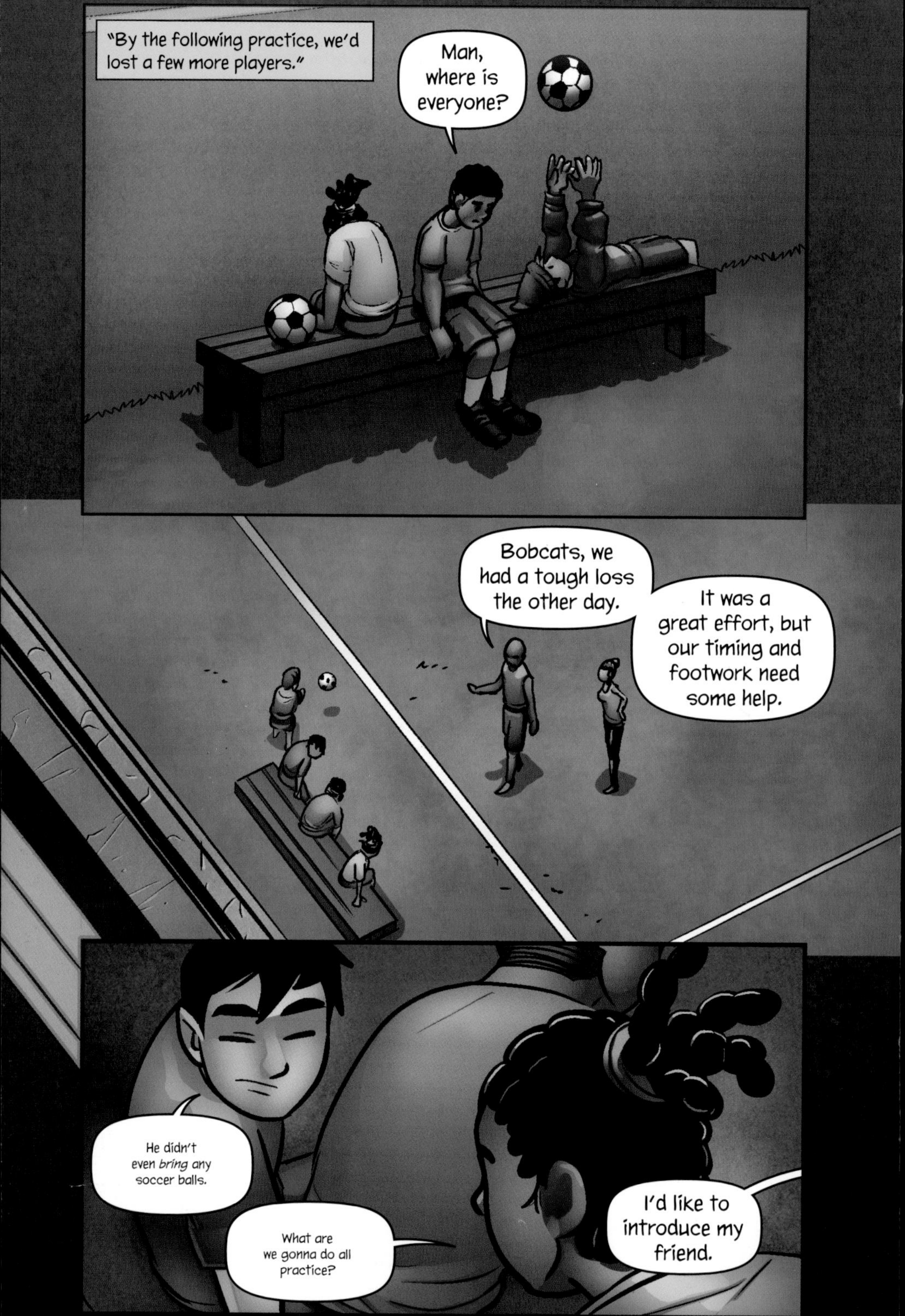
"By the following practice, we'd lost a few more players."
Man, where is everyone?
Bobcats, we had a tough loss the other day.
It was a great effort, but our timing and footwork need some help.
He didn't even *bring* any soccer balls.
What are we gonna do all practice?
I'd like to introduce my friend.

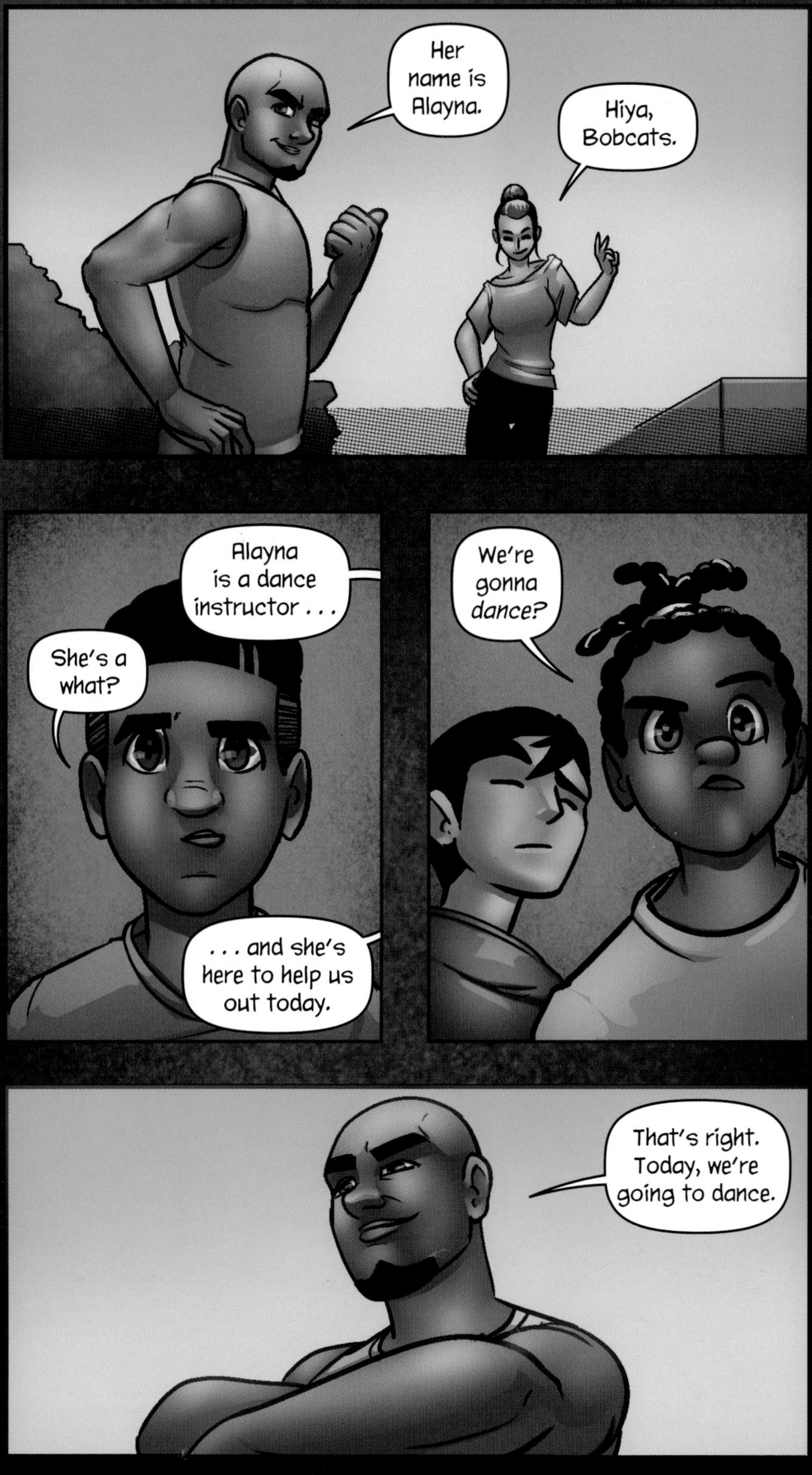
Her name is Alayna.
Hiya, Bobcats.
Alayna is a dance instructor . . .
She's a what?
. . . and she's here to help us out today.
We're gonna dance?
That's right. Today, we're going to dance.

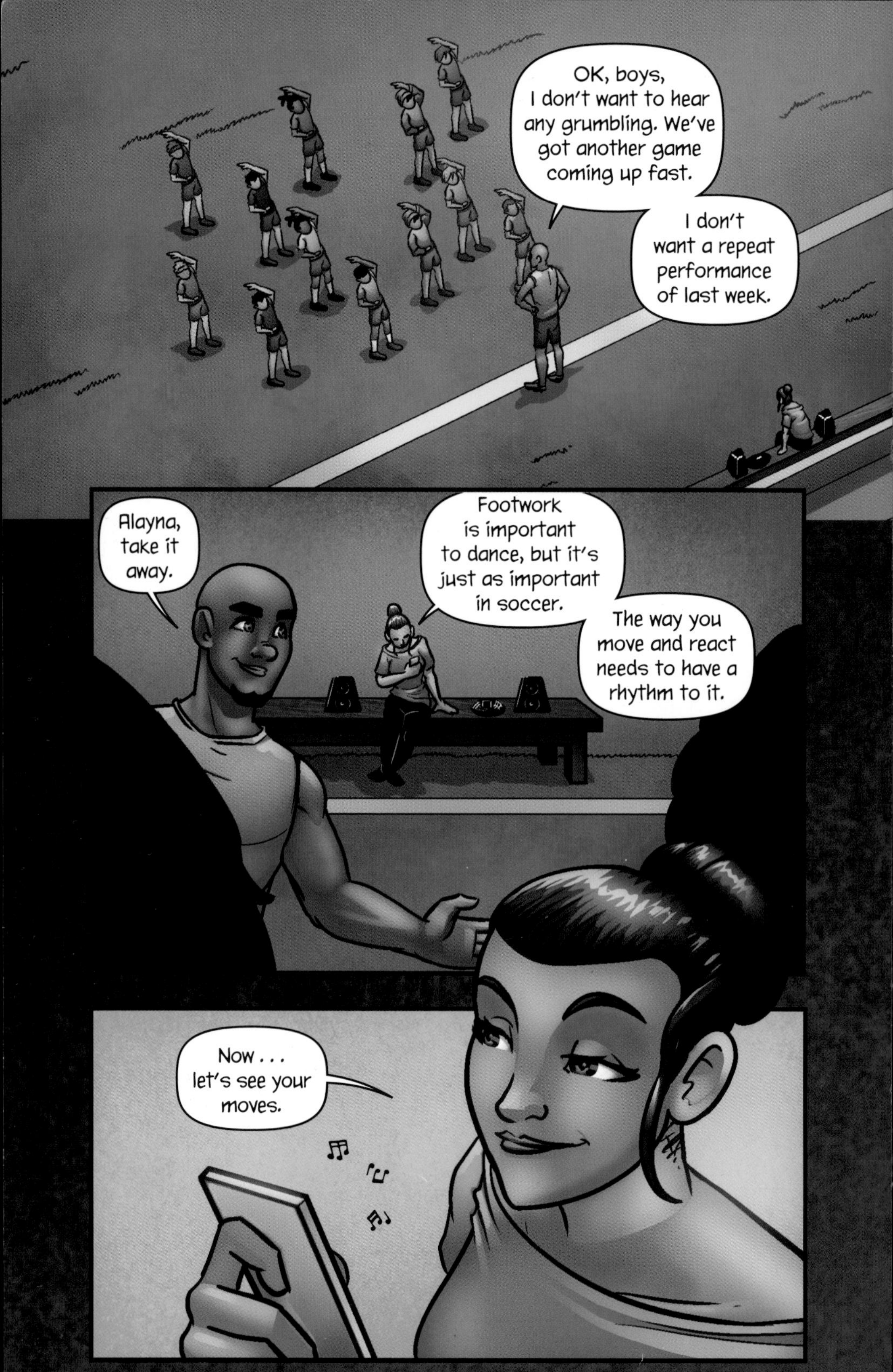
OK, boys, I don't want to hear any grumbling. We've got another game coming up fast.
I don't want a repeat performance of last week.
Alayna, take it away.
Footwork is important to dance, but it's just as important in soccer.
The way you move and react needs to have a rhythm to it.
Now . . . let's see your moves.

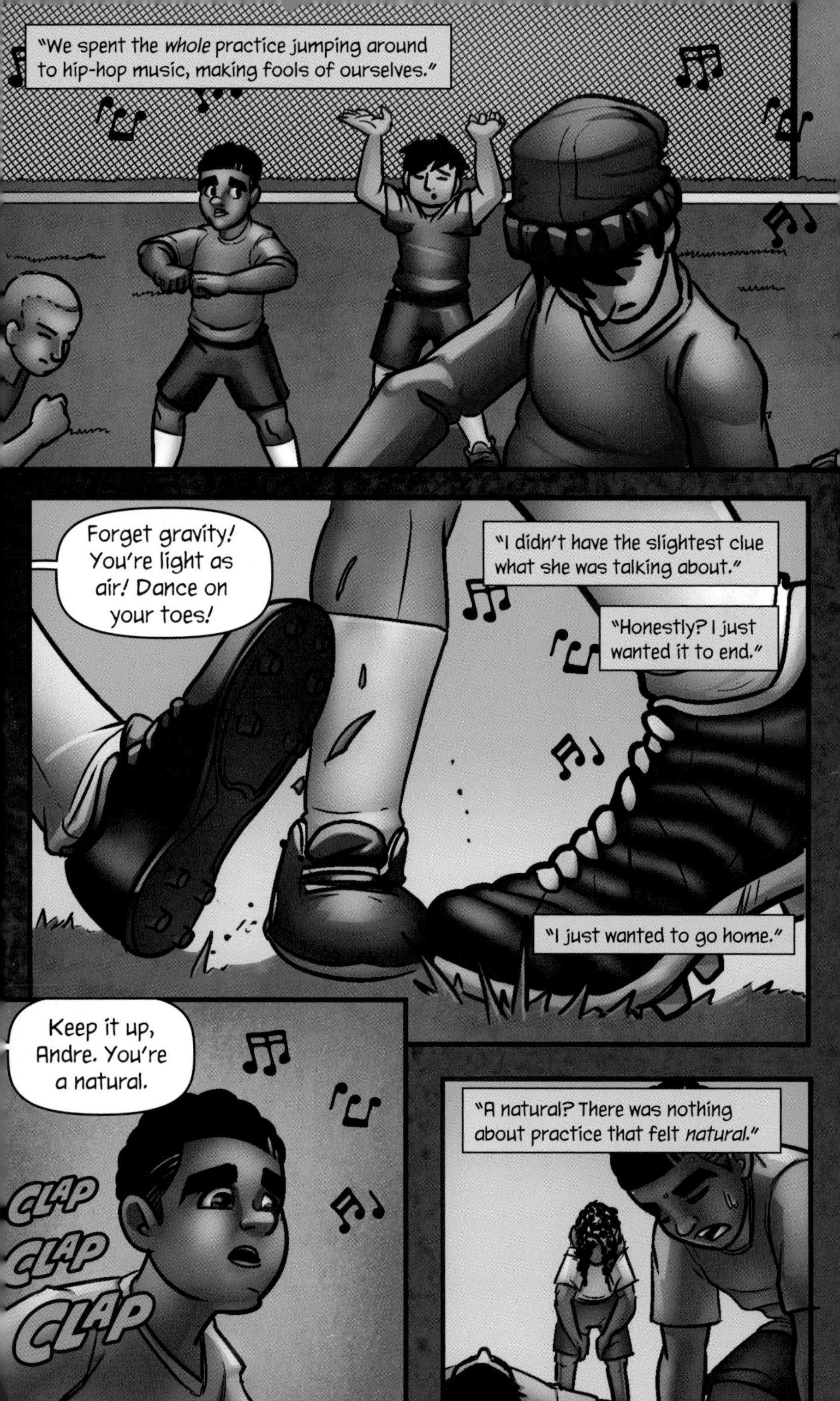

"We spent the *whole* practice jumping around to hip-hop music, making fools of ourselves."
Forget gravity! You're light as air! Dance on your toes!
"I didn't have the slightest clue what she was talking about."
"Honestly? I just wanted it to end."
"I just wanted to go home."
Keep it up, Andre. You're a natural.
CLAP
CLAP
CLAP
"A natural? There was nothing about practice that felt *natural.*"

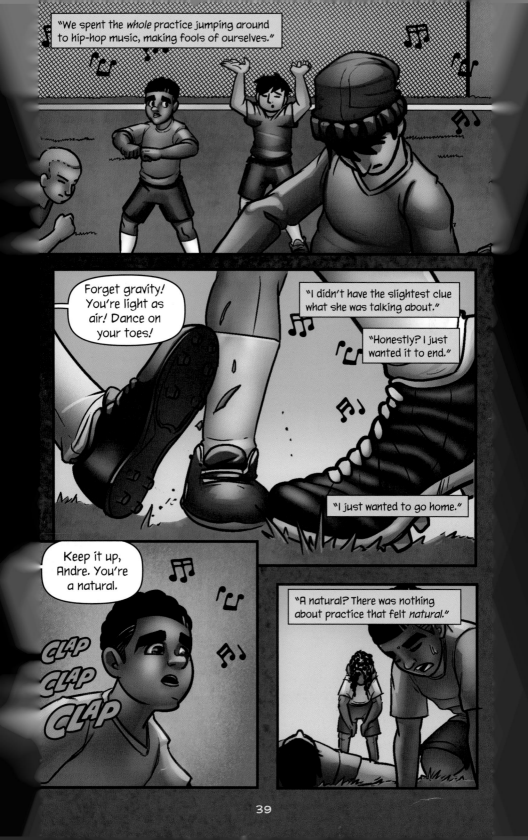

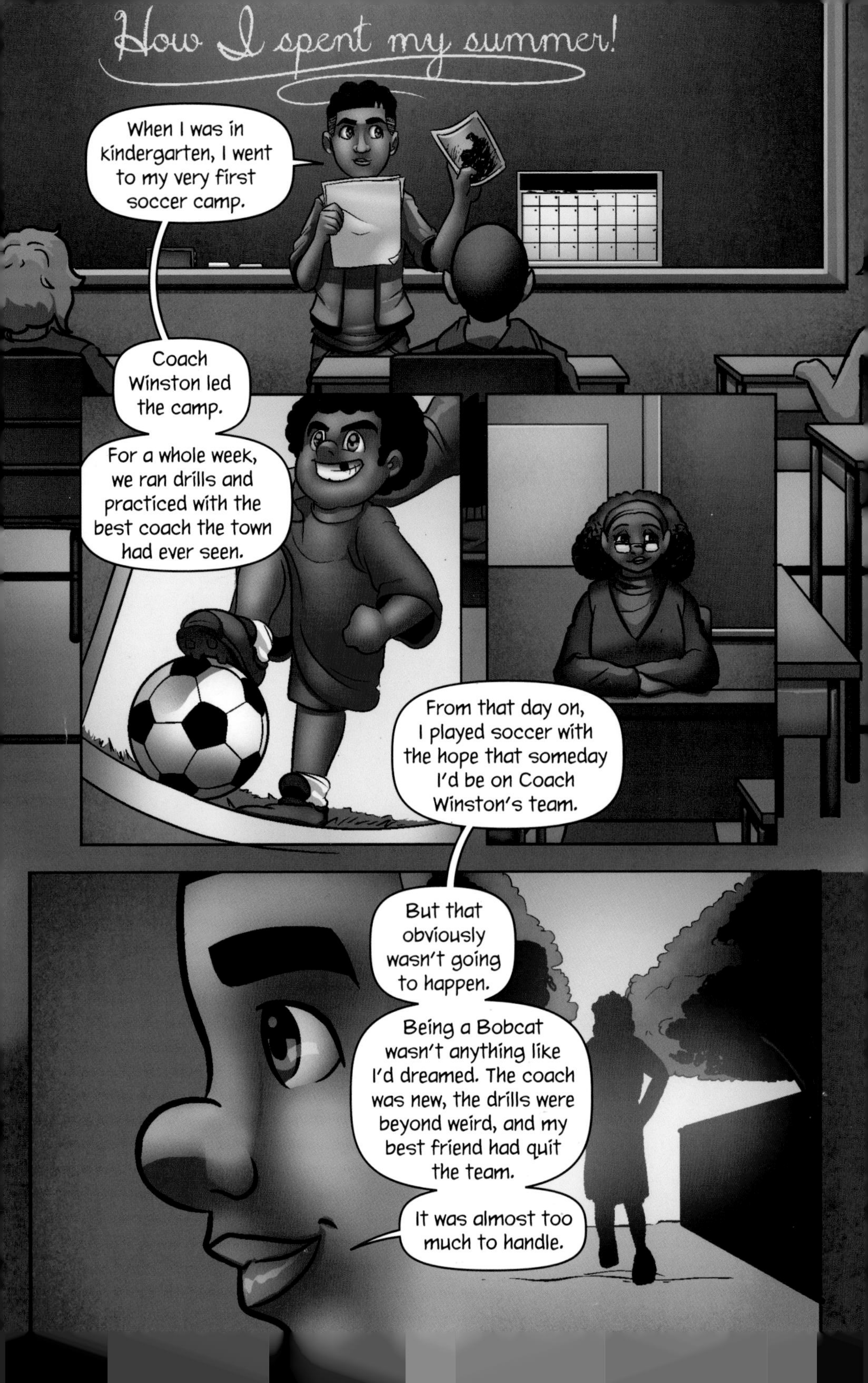

How I spent my summer!
When I was in kindergarten, I went to my very first soccer camp.
Coach Winston led the camp.
For a whole week, we ran drills and practiced with the best coach the town had ever seen.
From that day on, I played soccer with the hope that someday I'd be on Coach Winston's team.
But that obviously wasn't going to happen.
Being a Bobcat wasn't anything like I'd dreamed. The coach was new, the drills were beyond weird, and my best friend had quit the team.
It was almost too much to handle.

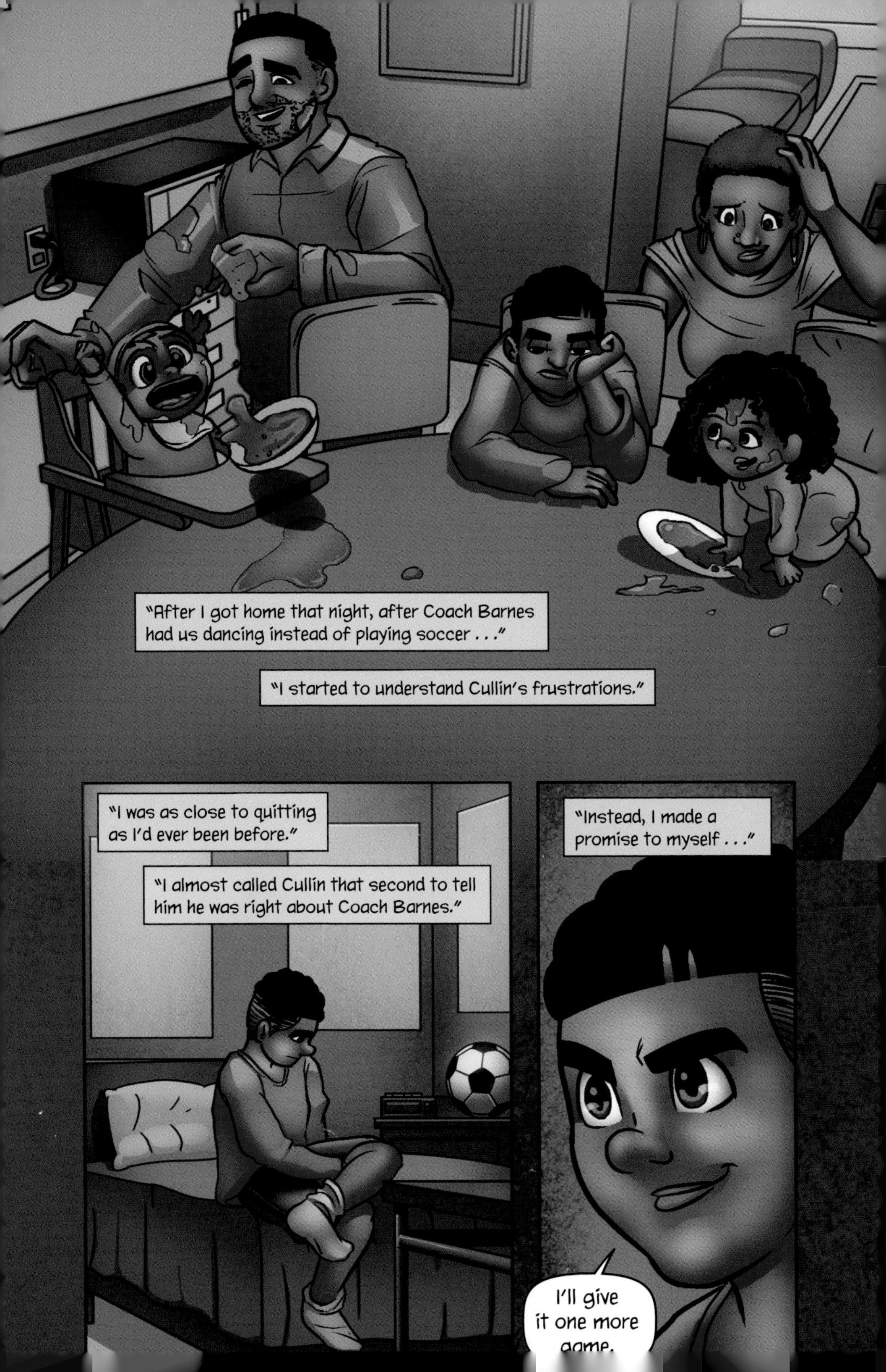
"After I got home that night, after Coach Barnes had us dancing instead of playing soccer . . ."
"I started to understand Cullin's frustrations."
"I was as close to quitting as I'd ever been before."
"I almost called Cullin that second to tell him he was right about Coach Barnes."
"Instead, I made a promise to myself . . ."
I'll give it one more game.

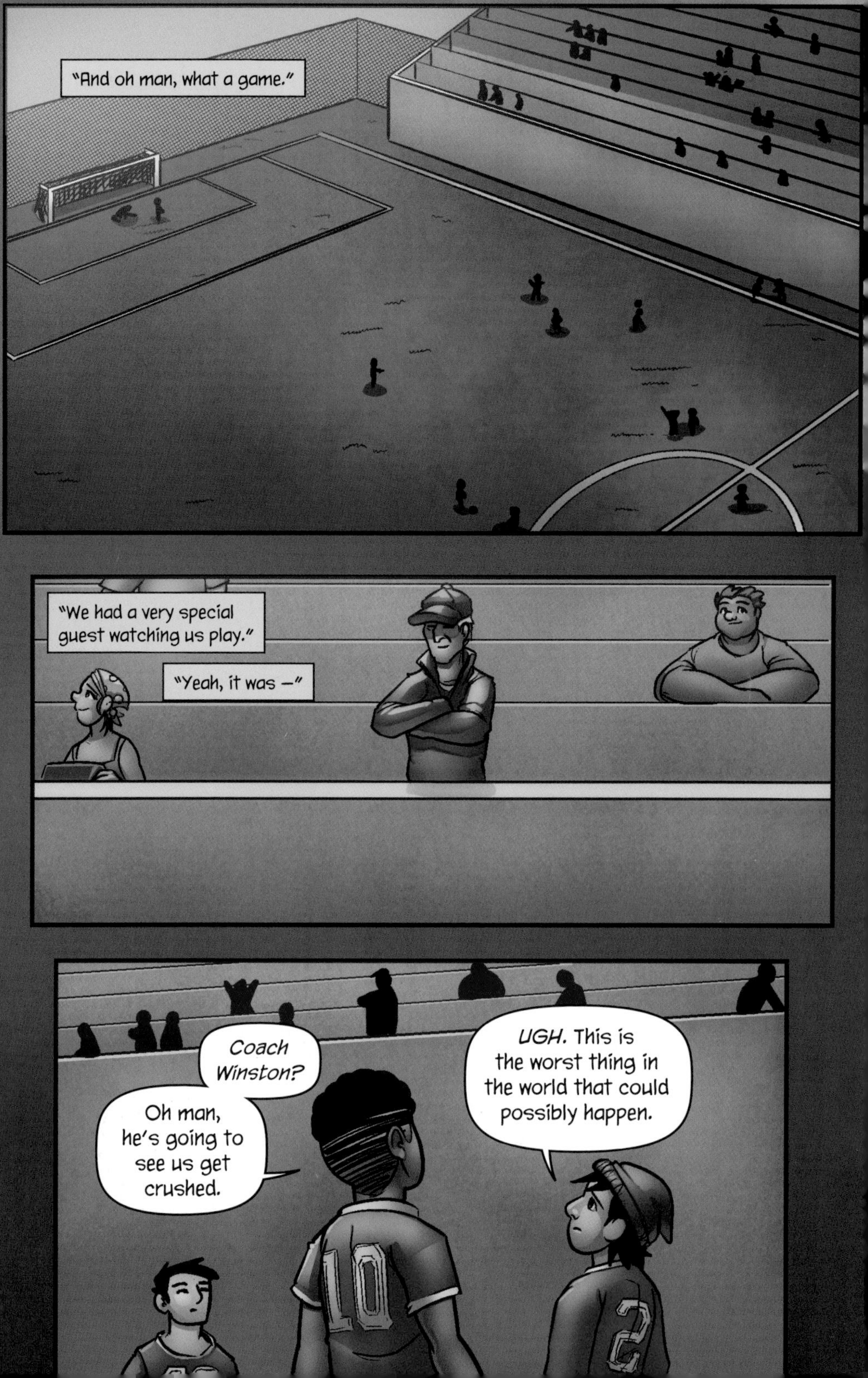
"And oh man, what a game."
"We had a very special guest watching us play."
"Yeah, it was —"
Coach Winston?
Oh man, he's going to see us get crushed.
UGH. This is the worst thing in the world that could possibly happen.

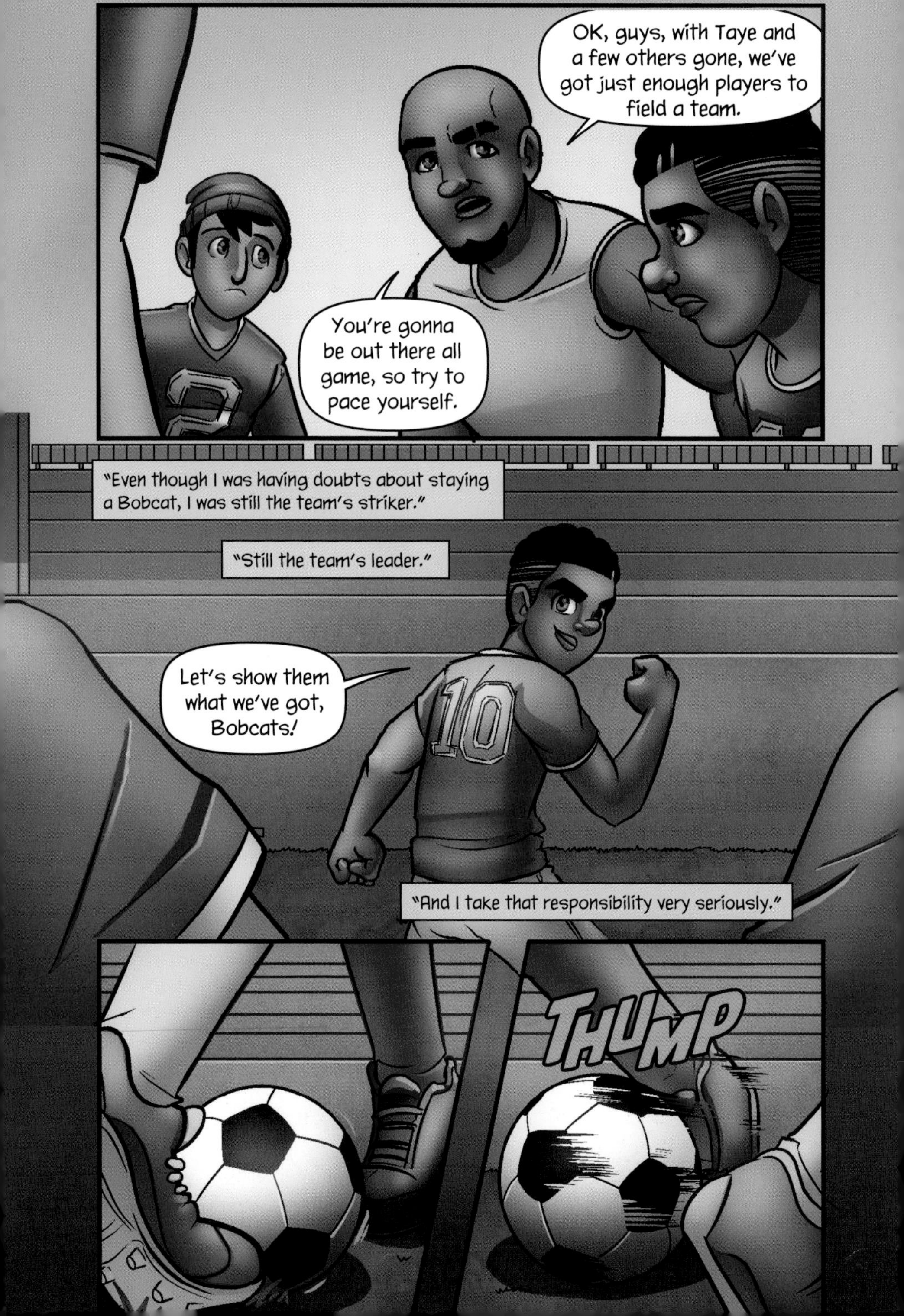
OK, guys, with Taye and a few others gone, we've got just enough players to field a team.
You're gonna be out there all game, so try to pace yourself.
"Even though I was having doubts about staying a Bobcat, I was still the team's striker."
"Still the team's leader."
Let's show them what we've got, Bobcats!
"And I take that responsibility very seriously."
THUMP

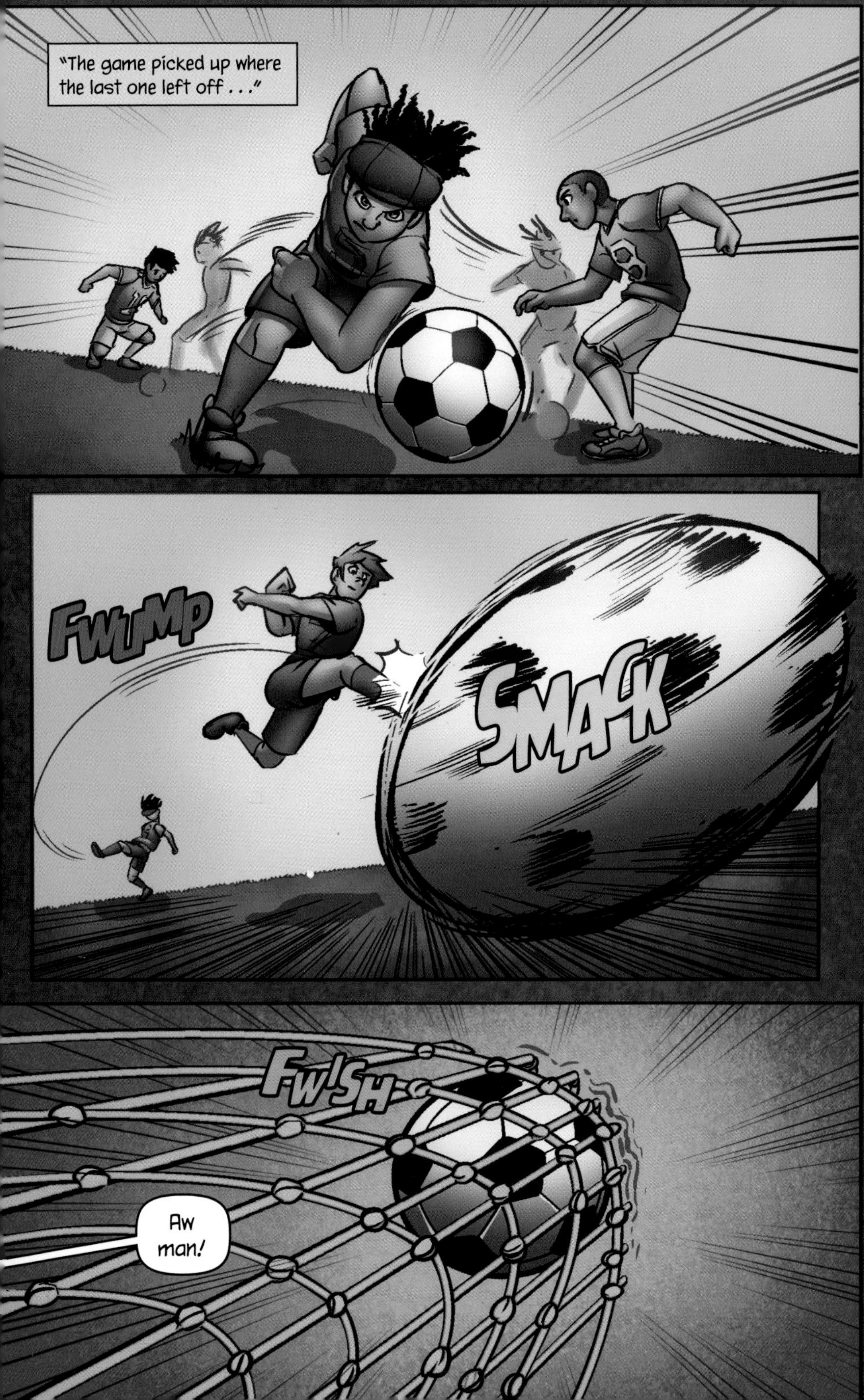
"The game picked up where the last one left off . . ."
FWUMP
SMACK
FWISH
Aw man!

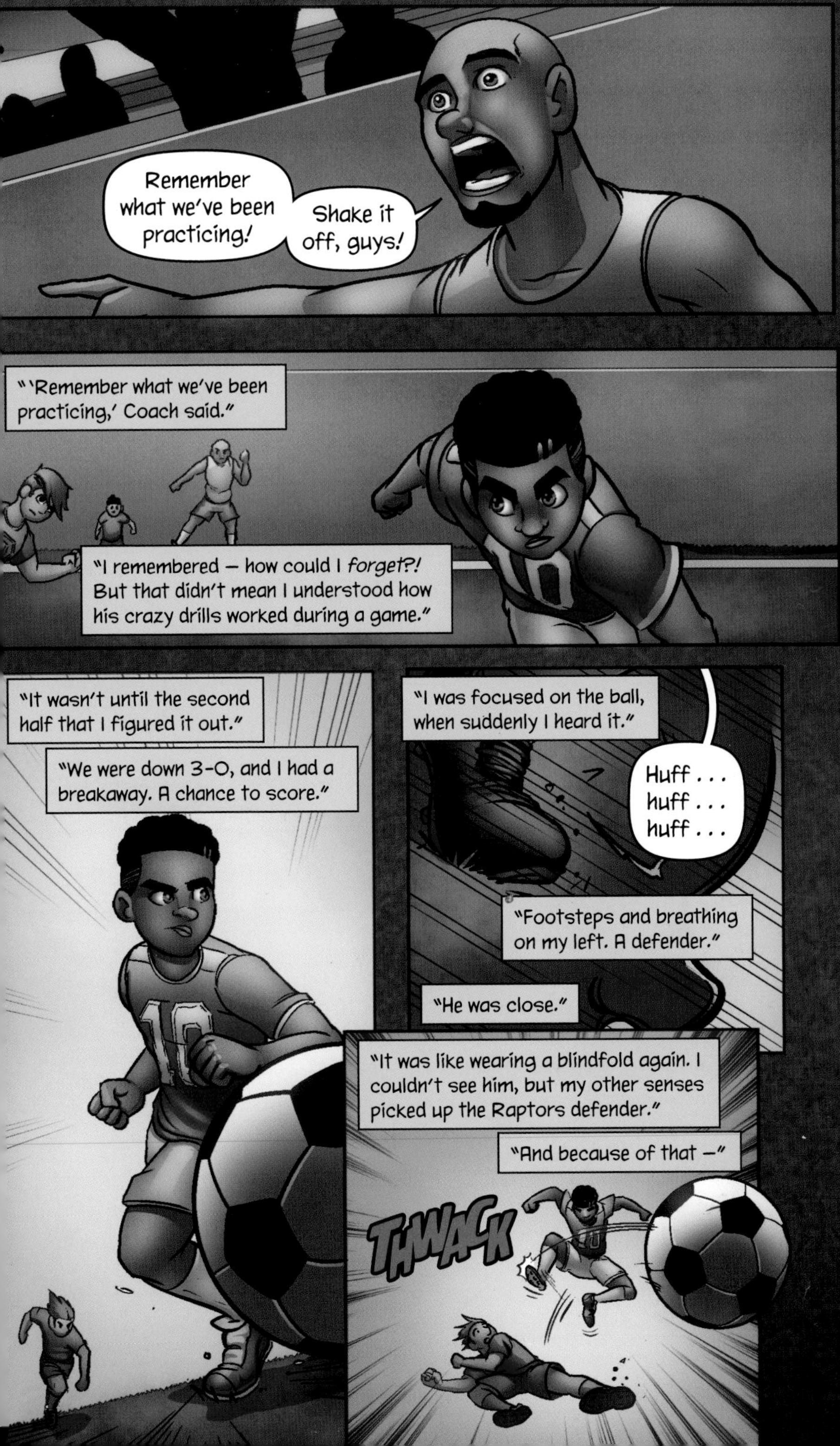
Remember what we've been practicing!
Shake it off, guys!
"'Remember what we've been practicing,' Coach said."
"I remembered — how could I *forget*?! But that didn't mean I understood how his crazy drills worked during a game."
"It wasn't until the second half that I figured it out."
"We were down 3-0, and I had a breakaway. A chance to score."
"I was focused on the ball, when suddenly I heard it."
Huff . . . huff . . . huff . . .
"Footsteps and breathing on my left. A defender."
"He was close."
"It was like wearing a blindfold again. I couldn't see him, but my other senses picked up the Raptors defender."
"And because of that —"
THWACK

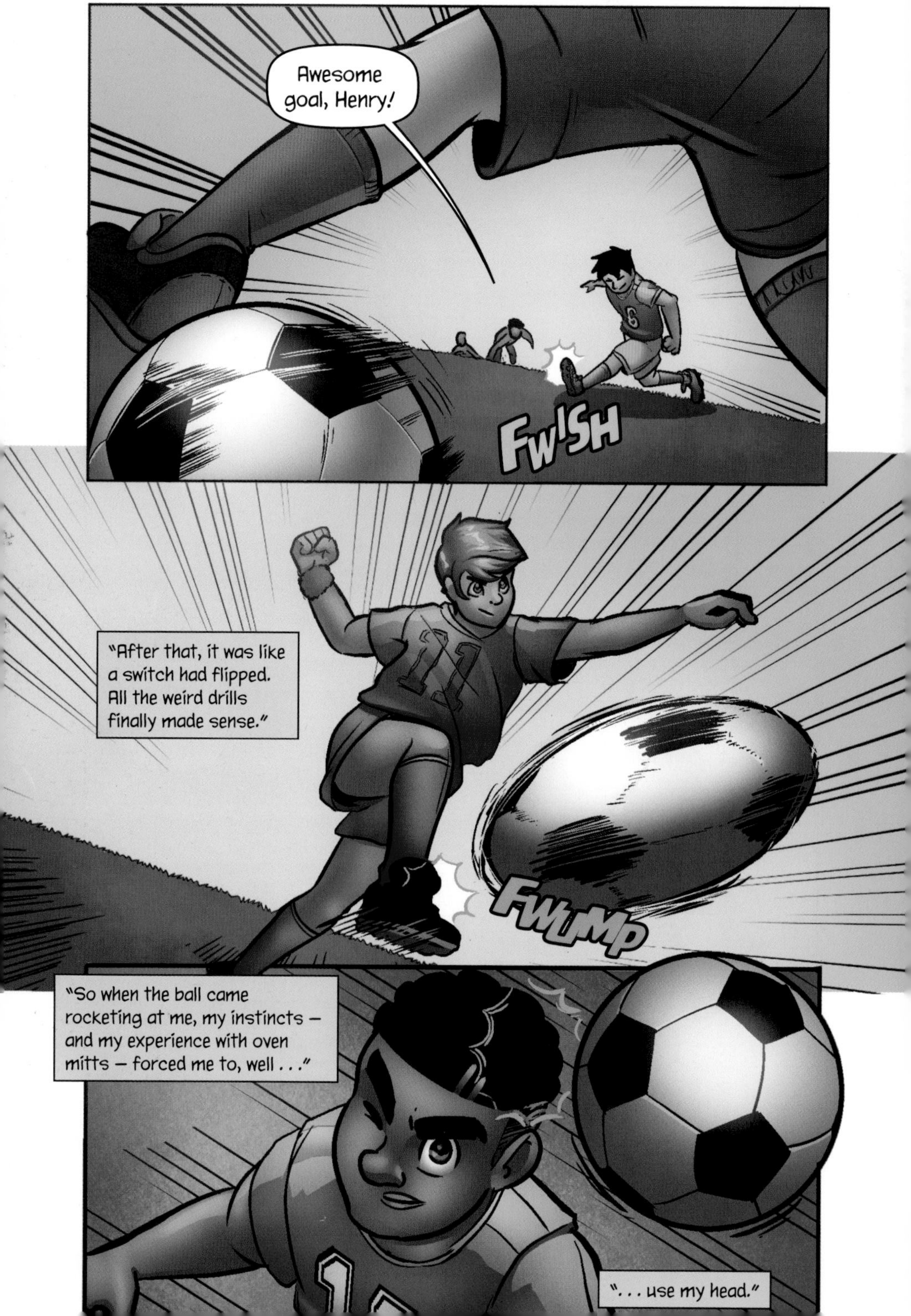
Awesome goal, Henry!
FWISH
"After that, it was like a switch had flipped. All the weird drills finally made sense."
FWUMP
"So when the ball came rocketing at me, my instincts — and my experience with oven mitts — forced me to, well . . ."
". . . use my head."

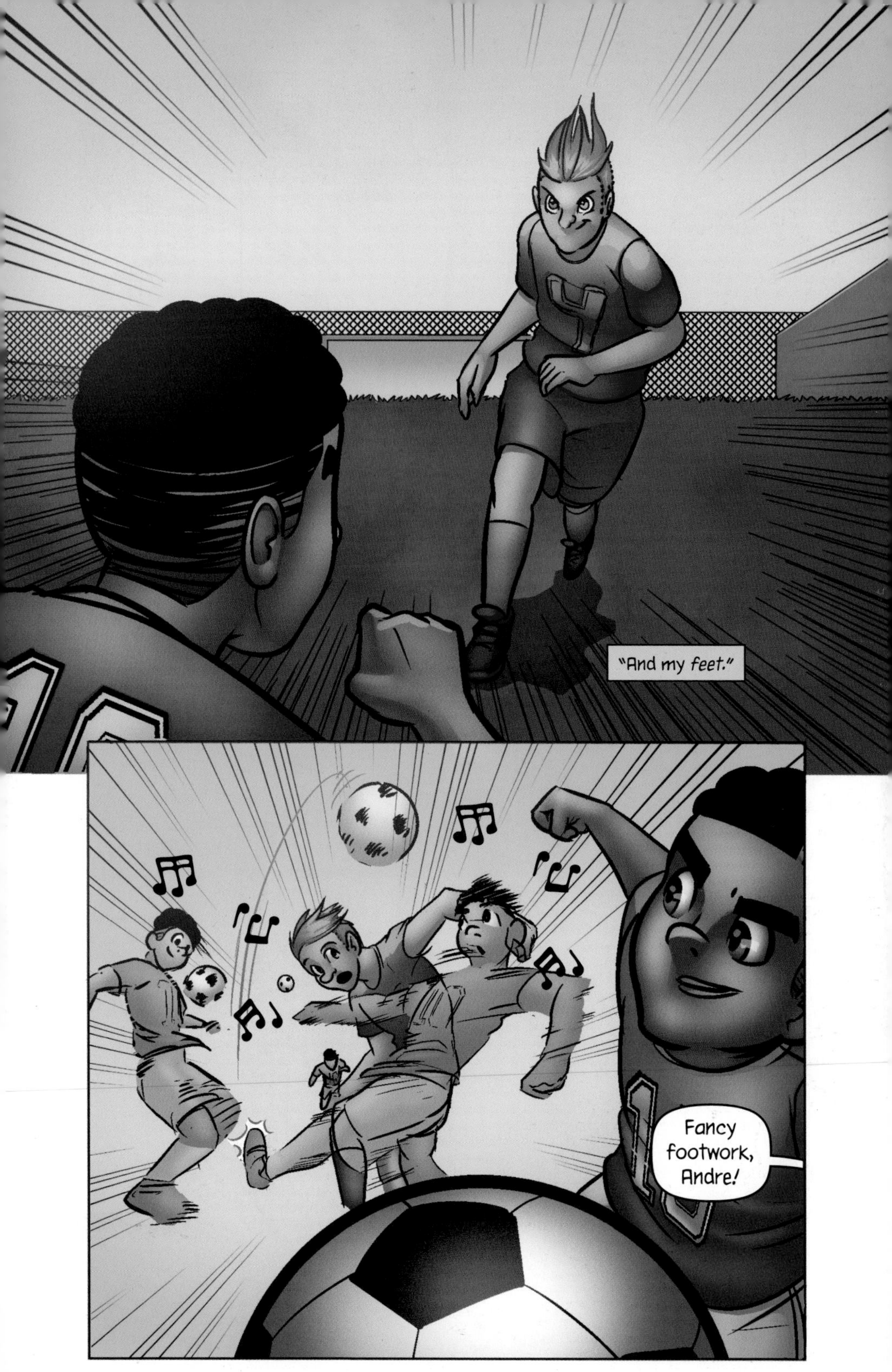
"And my *feet*."
Fancy footwork, Andre!

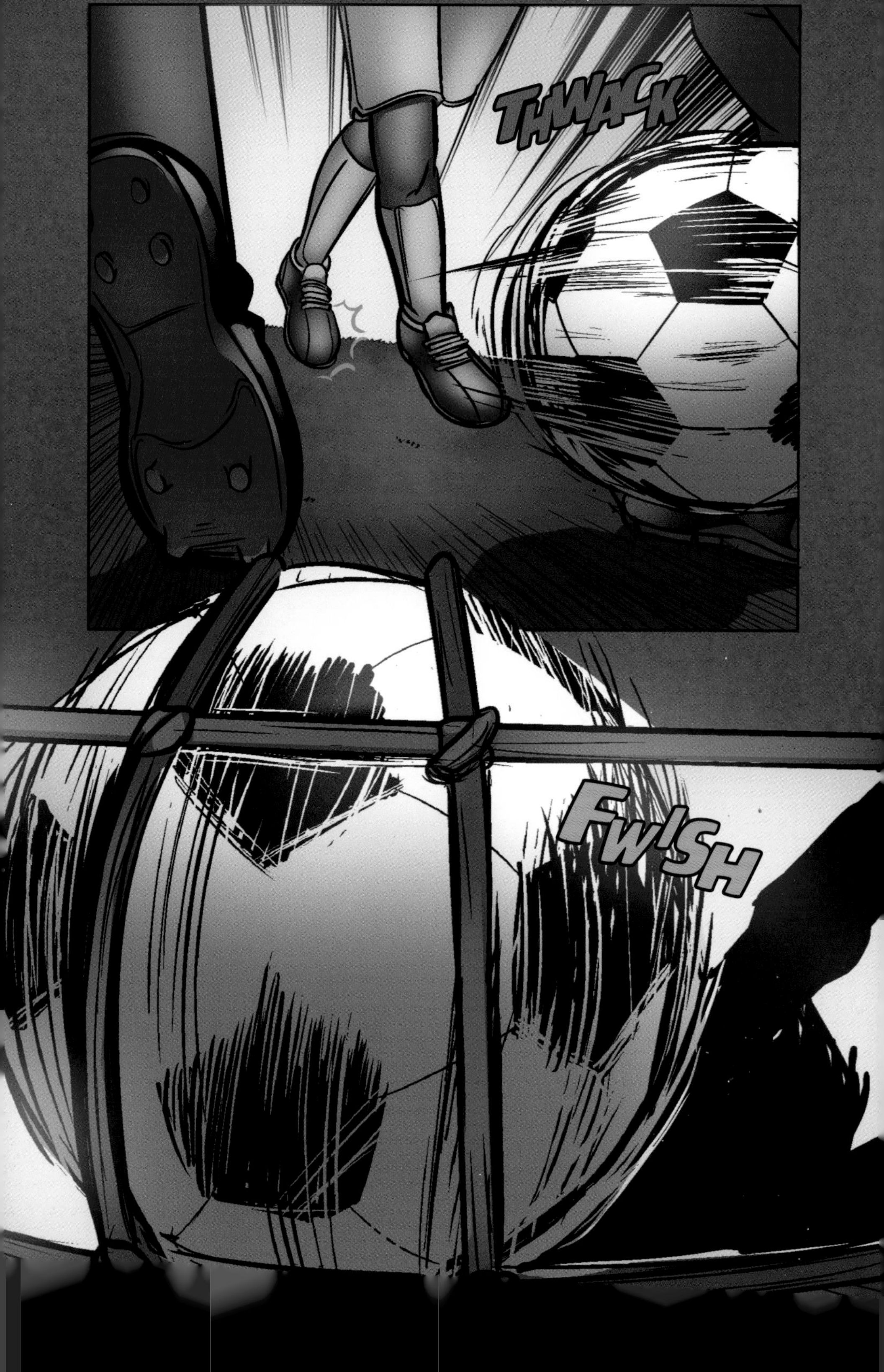
THWACK
FW'SH

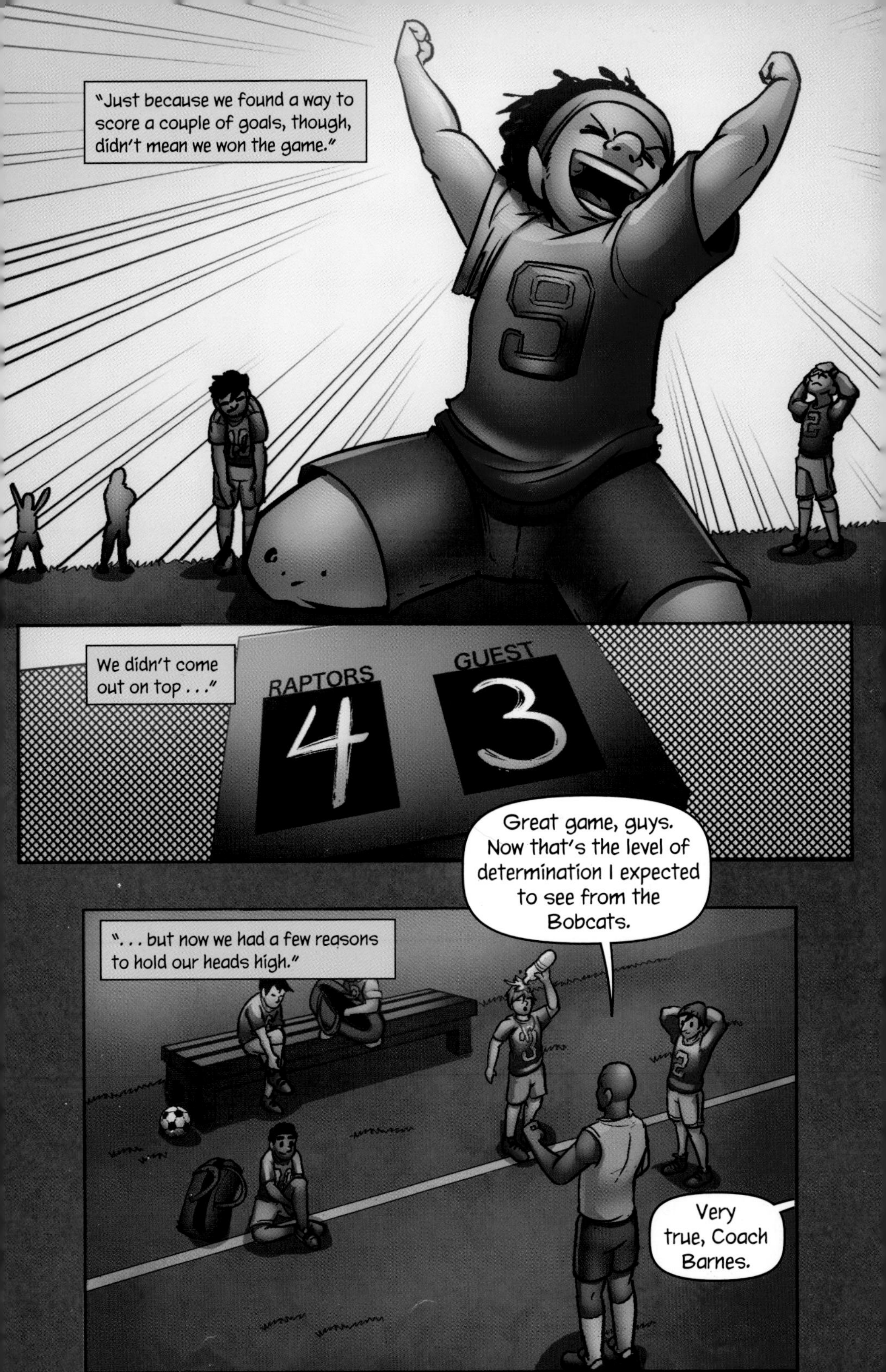
"Just because we found a way to score a couple of goals, though, didn't mean we won the game."
We didn't come out on top . . ."
RAPTORS
GUEST
4
3
Great game, guys. Now that's the level of determination I expected to see from the Bobcats.
". . . but now we had a few reasons to hold our heads high."
Very true, Coach Barnes.

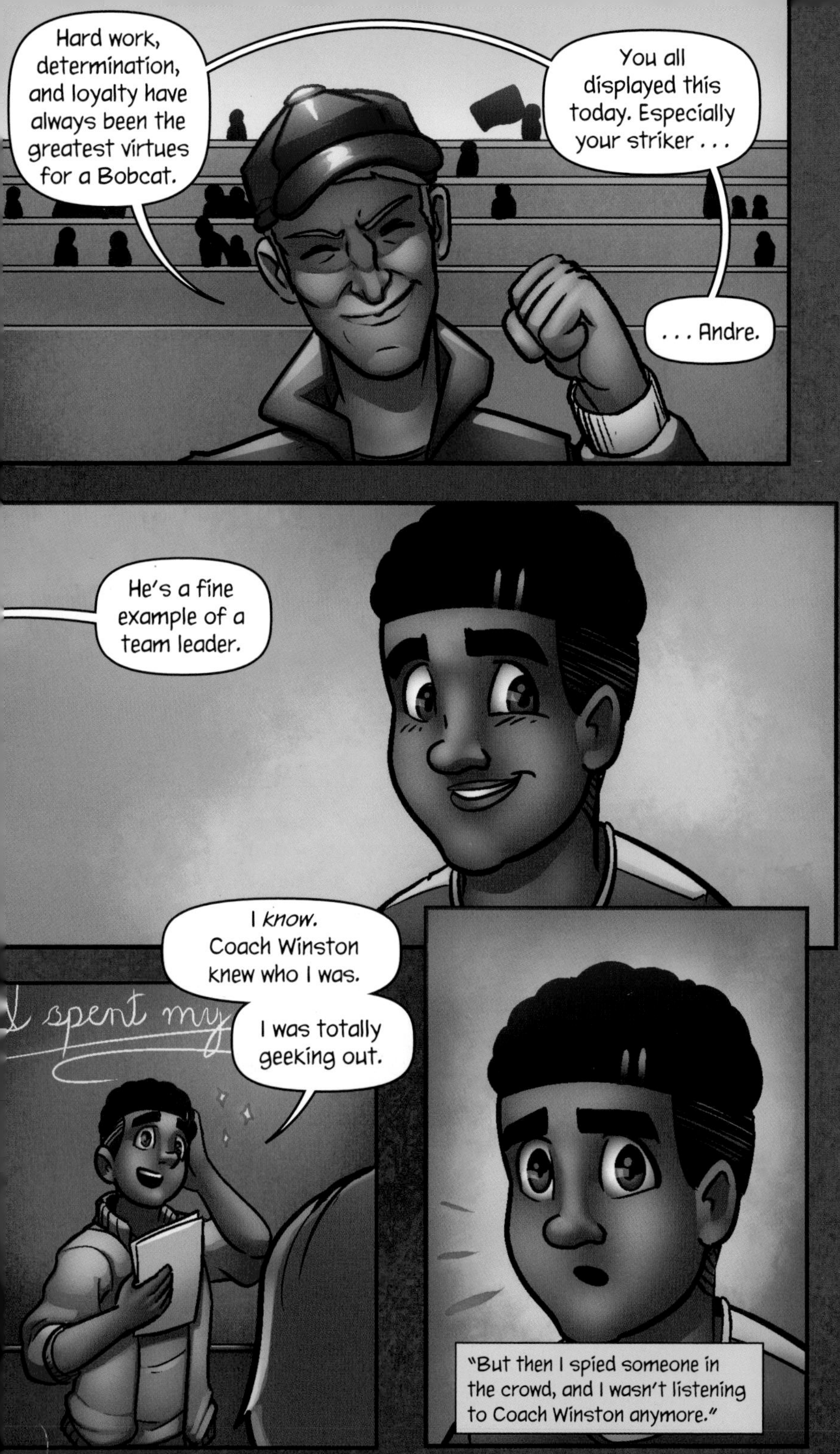
Hard work, determination, and loyalty have always been the greatest virtues for a Bobcat.
You all displayed this today. Especially your striker . . .
. . . Andre.
He's a fine example of a team leader.
I *know*. Coach Winston knew who I was.
I spent my
I was totally geeking out.
"But then I spied someone in the crowd, and I wasn't listening to Coach Winston anymore."

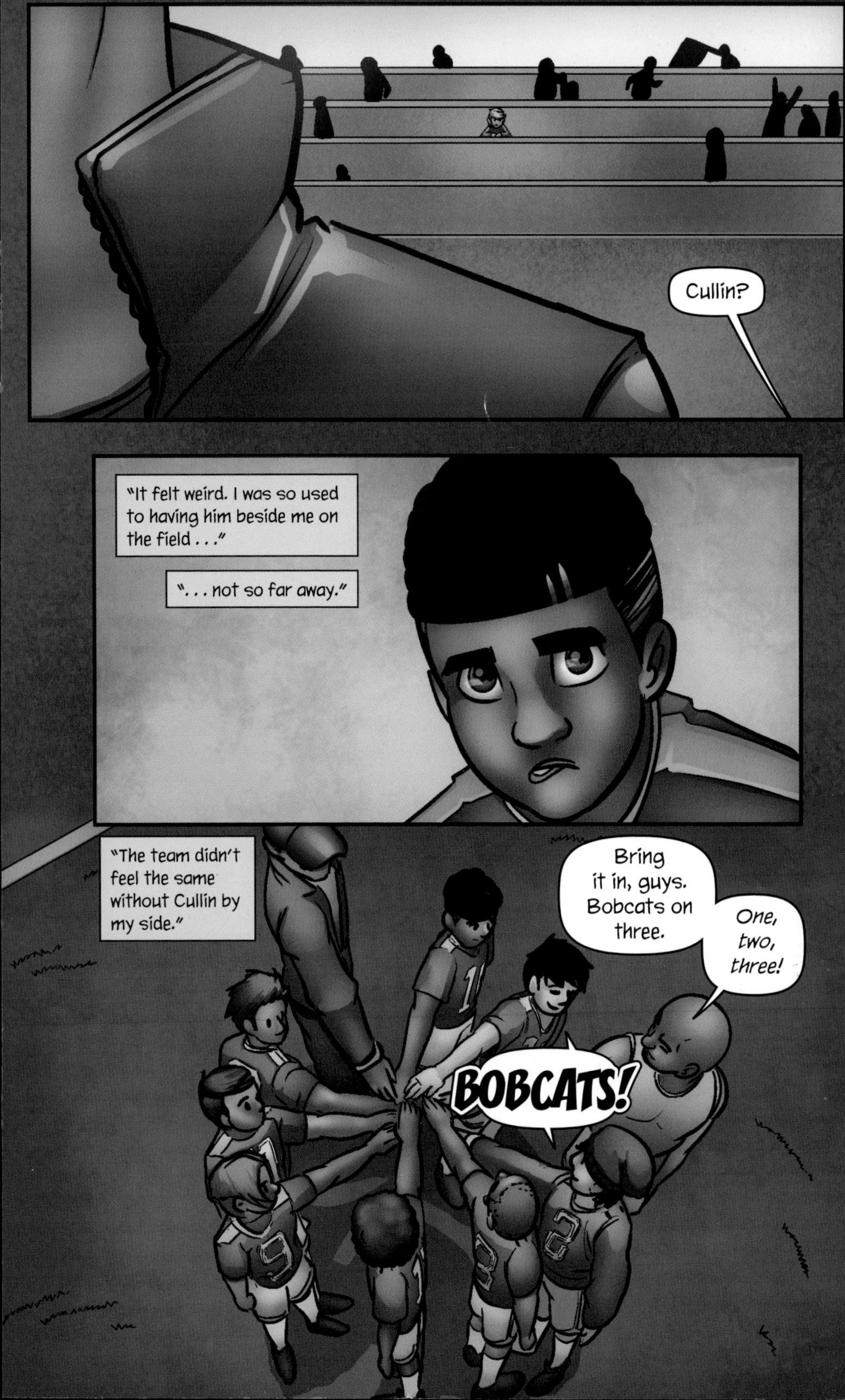
Cullin?
"It felt weird. I was so used to having him beside me on the field . . ."
". . . not so far away."
"The team didn't feel the same without Cullin by my side."
Bring it in, guys. Bobcats on three.
One, two, three!
BOBCATS!

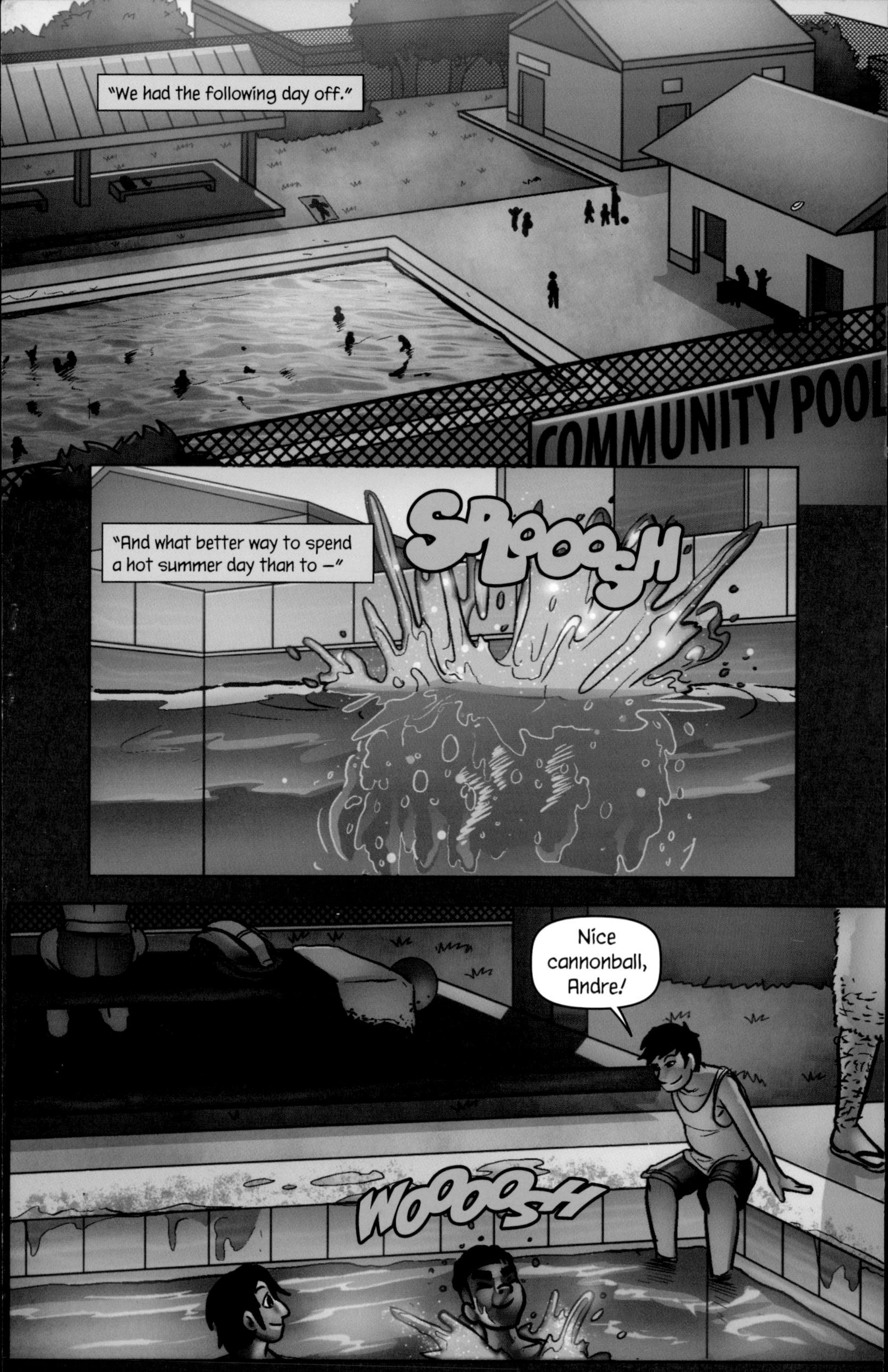
"We had the following day off."
COMMUNITY POOL
"And what better way to spend a hot summer day than to –"
SPLOOOSH
Nice cannonball, Andre!
WOOOSH

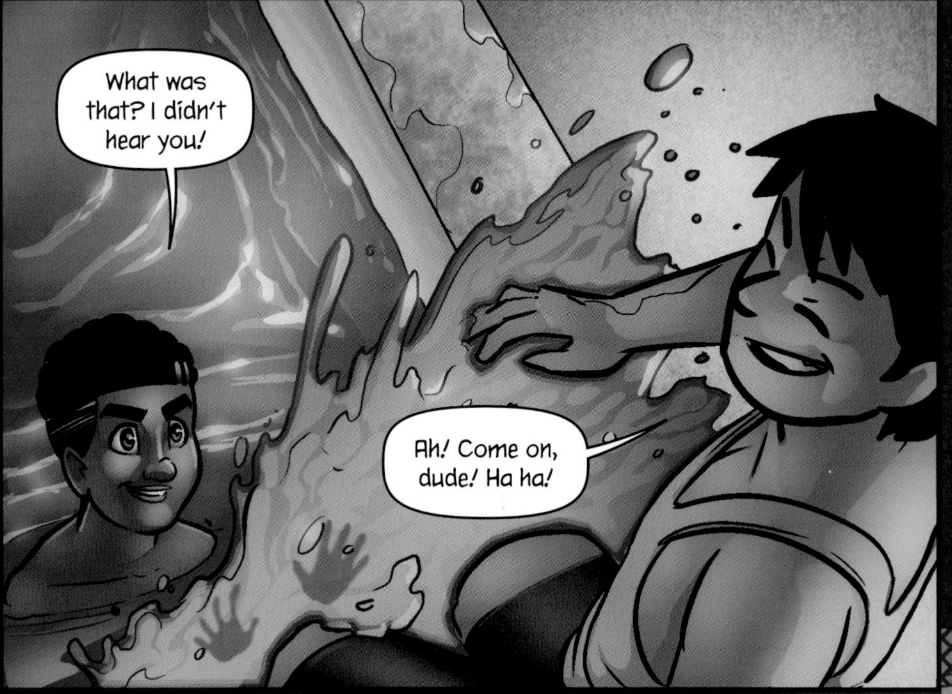
What was that? I didn't hear you!
Ah! Come on, dude! Ha ha!

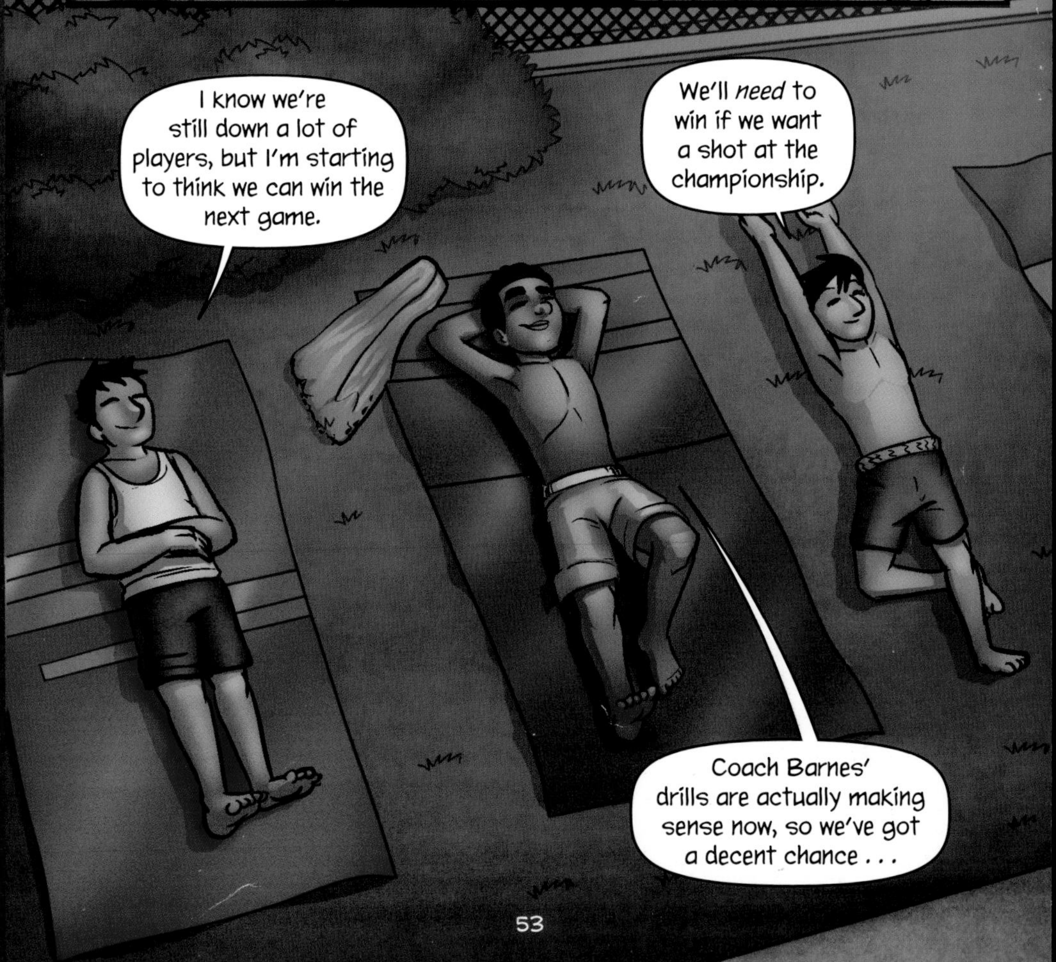
I know we're still down a lot of players, but I'm starting to think we can win the next game.
We'll *need* to win if we want a shot at the championship.
Coach Barnes' drills are actually making sense now, so we've got a decent chance . . .

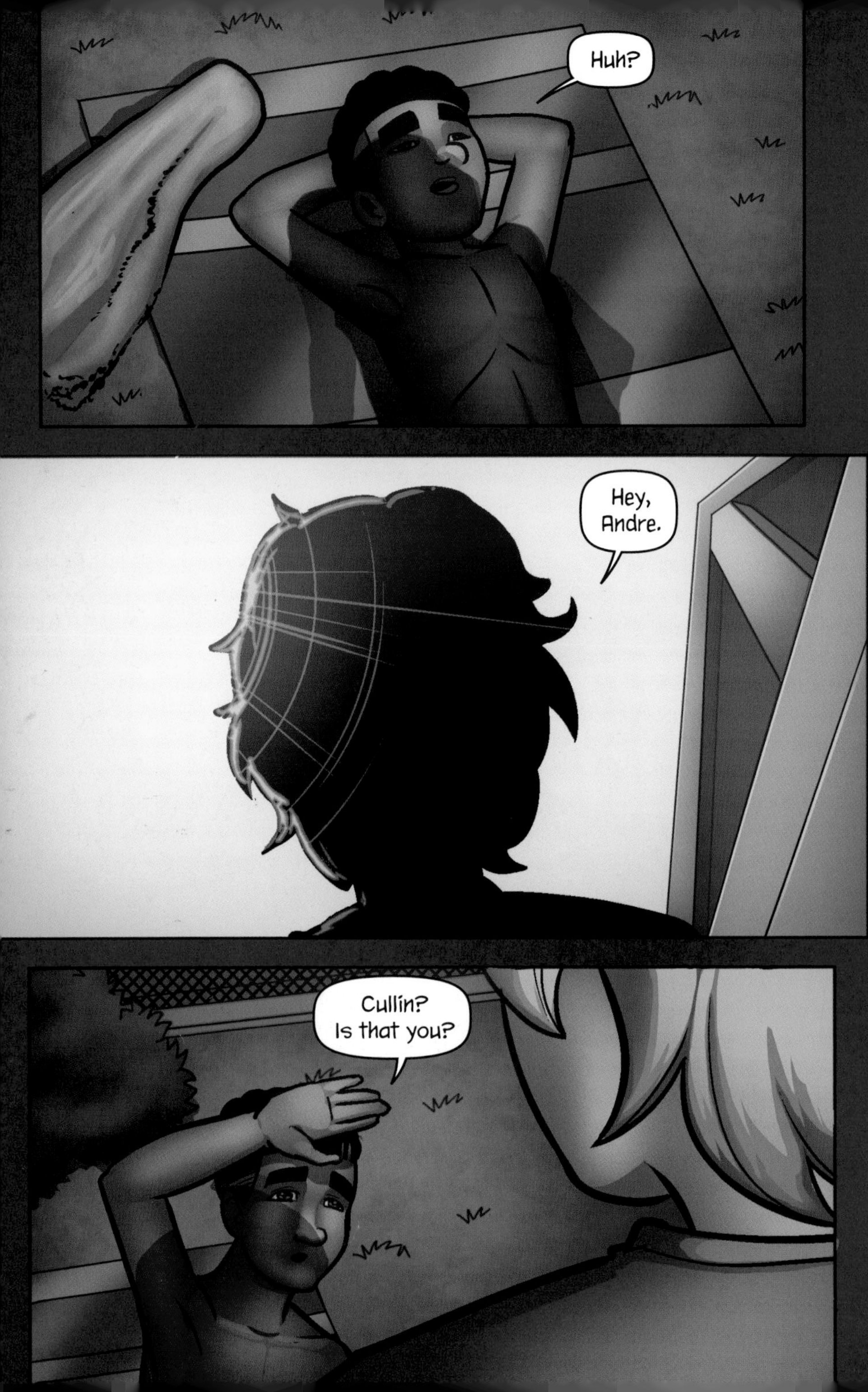
Huh?
Hey, Andre.
Cullin? Is that you?

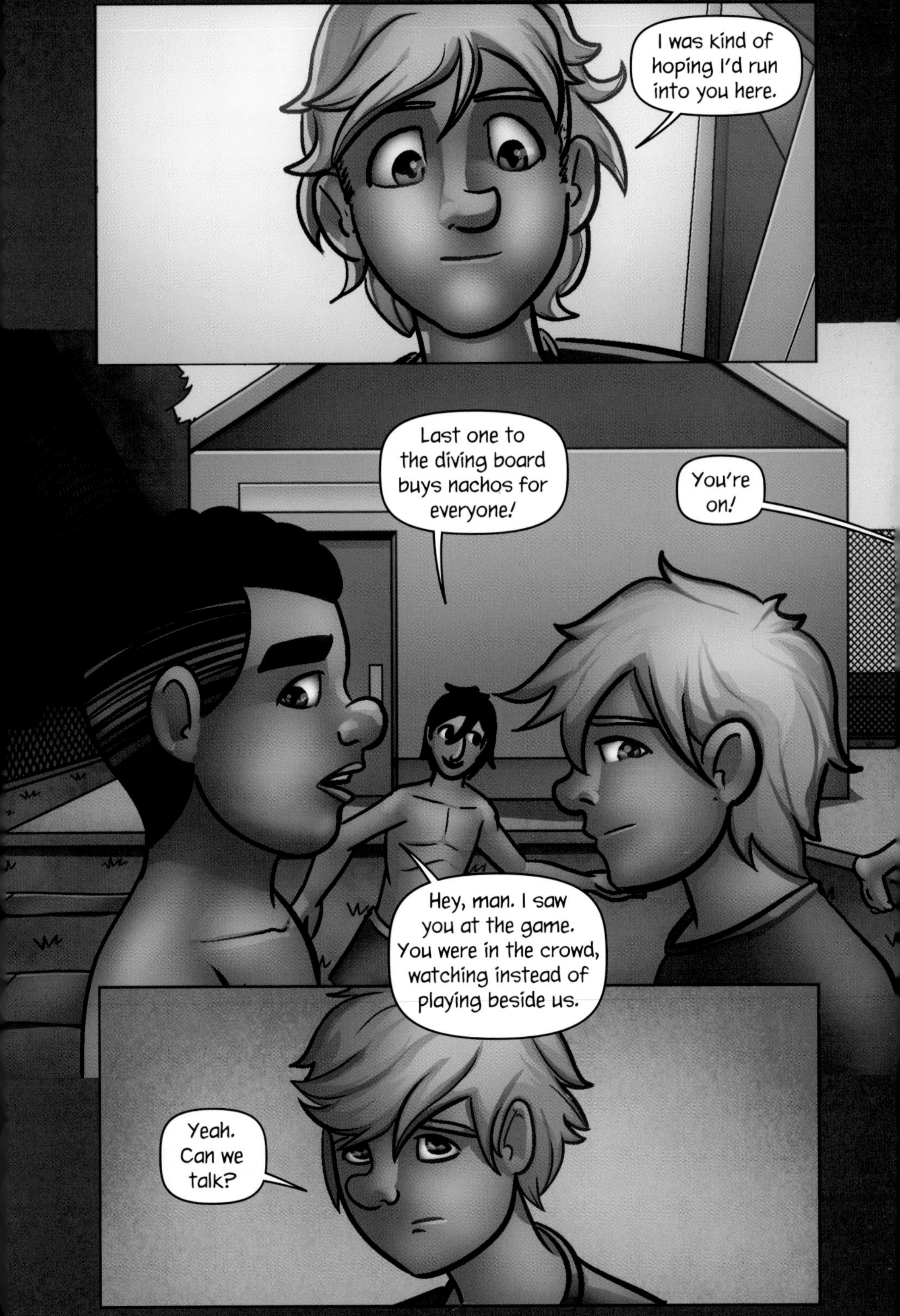

I was kind of hoping I'd run into you here.
Last one to the diving board buys nachos for everyone!
You're on!
Hey, man. I saw you at the game. You were in the crowd, watching instead of playing beside us.
Yeah. Can we talk?

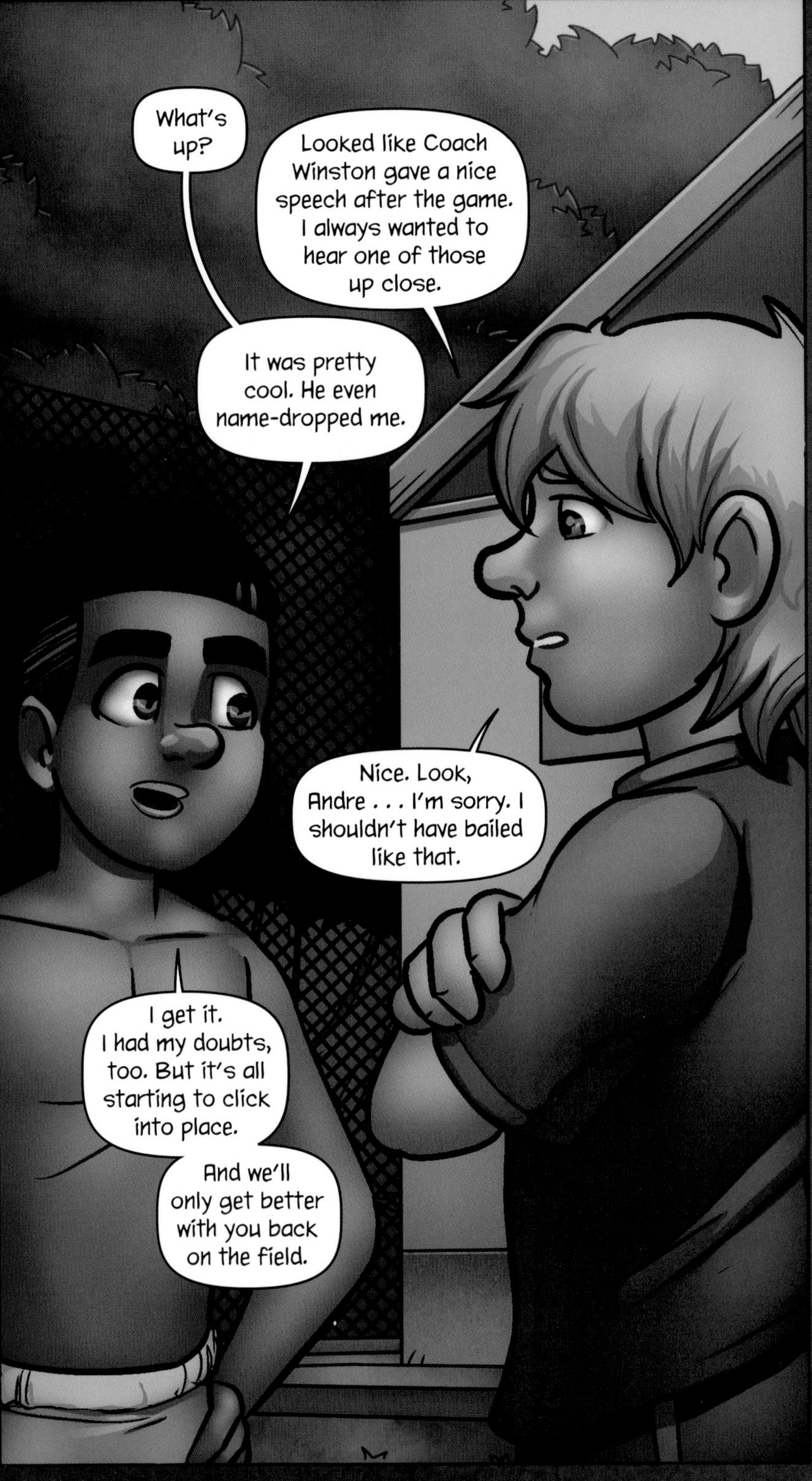
What's up?
Looked like Coach Winston gave a nice speech after the game. I always wanted to hear one of those up close.
It was pretty cool. He even name-dropped me.
Nice. Look, Andre . . . I'm sorry. I shouldn't have bailed like that.
I get it. I had my doubts, too. But it's all starting to click into place.
And we'll only get better with you back on the field.

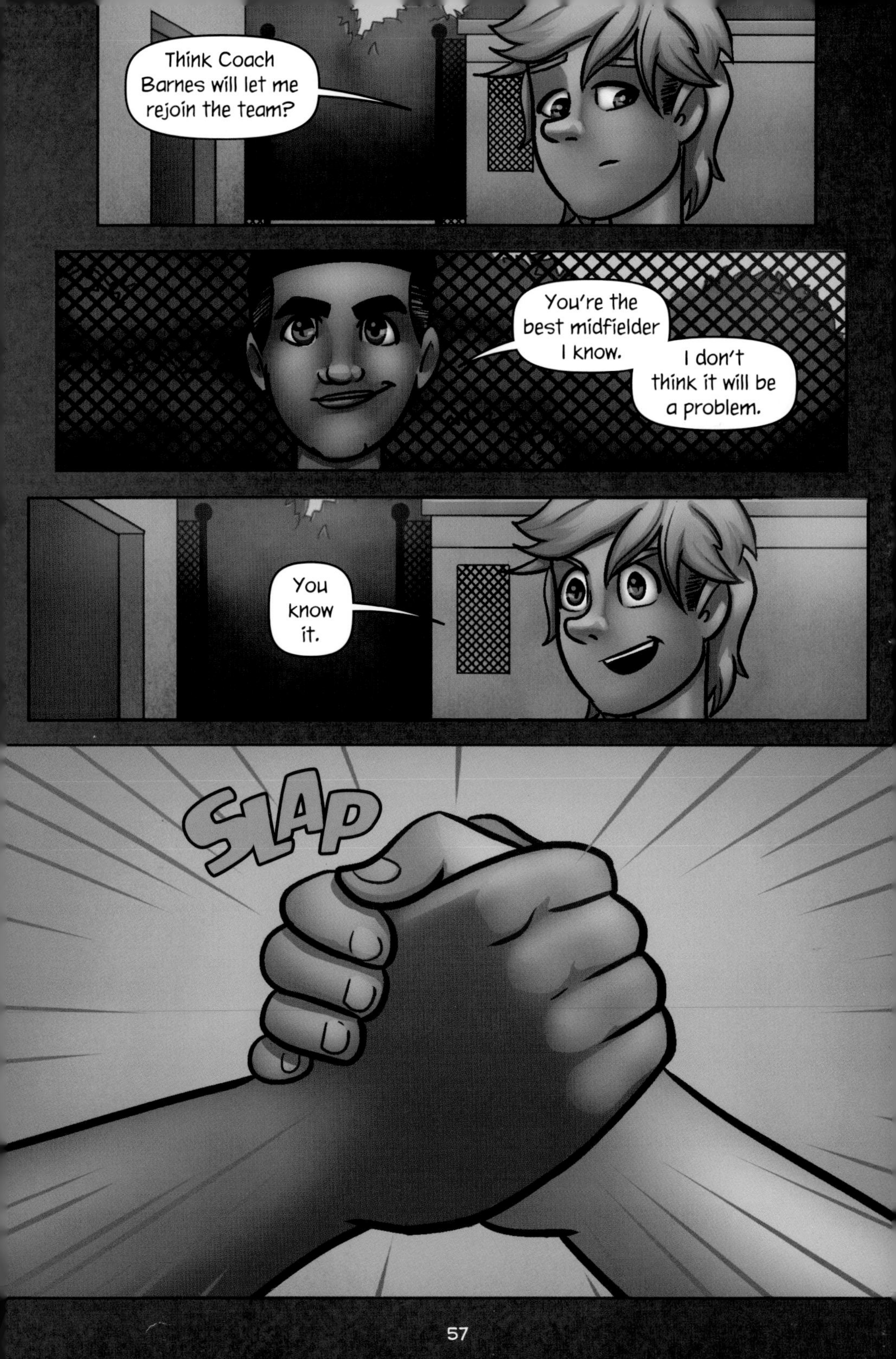

Think Coach Barnes will let me rejoin the team?
You're the best midfielder I know.
I don't think it will be a problem.
You know it.
SLAP

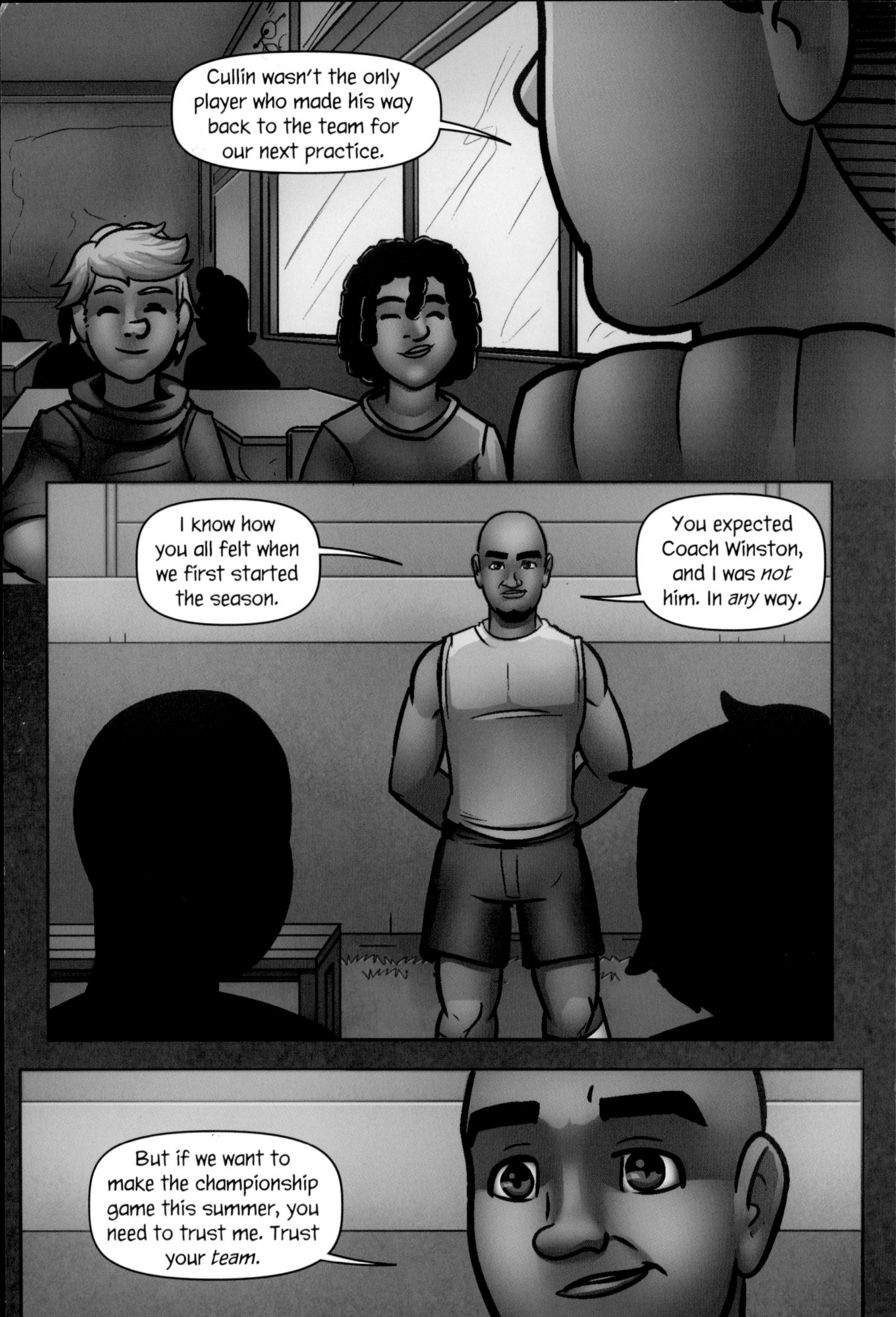
Cullin wasn't the only player who made his way back to the team for our next practice.
I know how you all felt when we first started the season.
You expected Coach Winston, and I was *not* him. In *any* way.
But if we want to make the championship game this summer, you need to trust me. Trust your *team*.

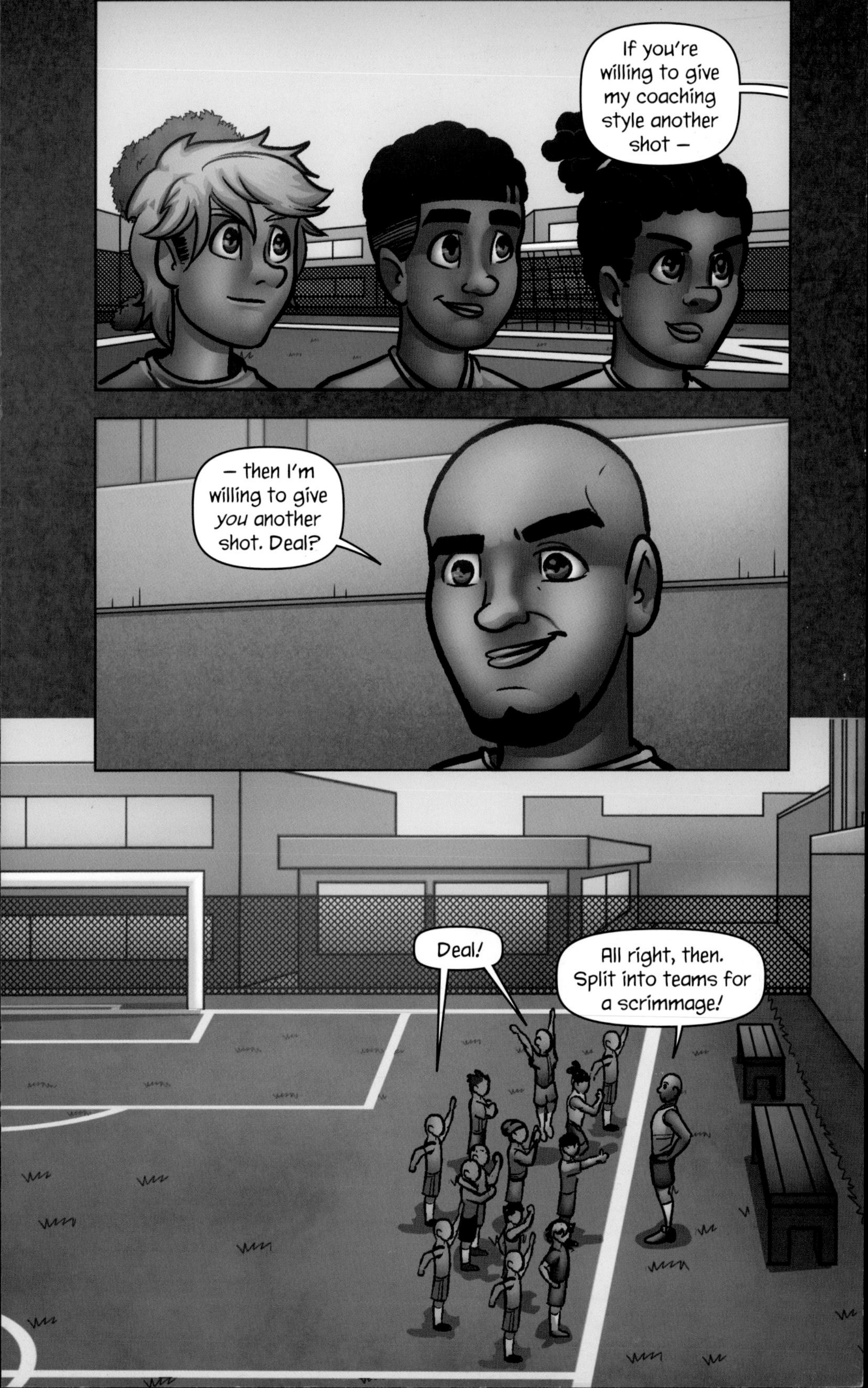
If you're willing to give my coaching style another shot –
– then I'm willing to give *you* another shot. Deal?
Deal!
All right, then. Split into teams for a scrimmage!

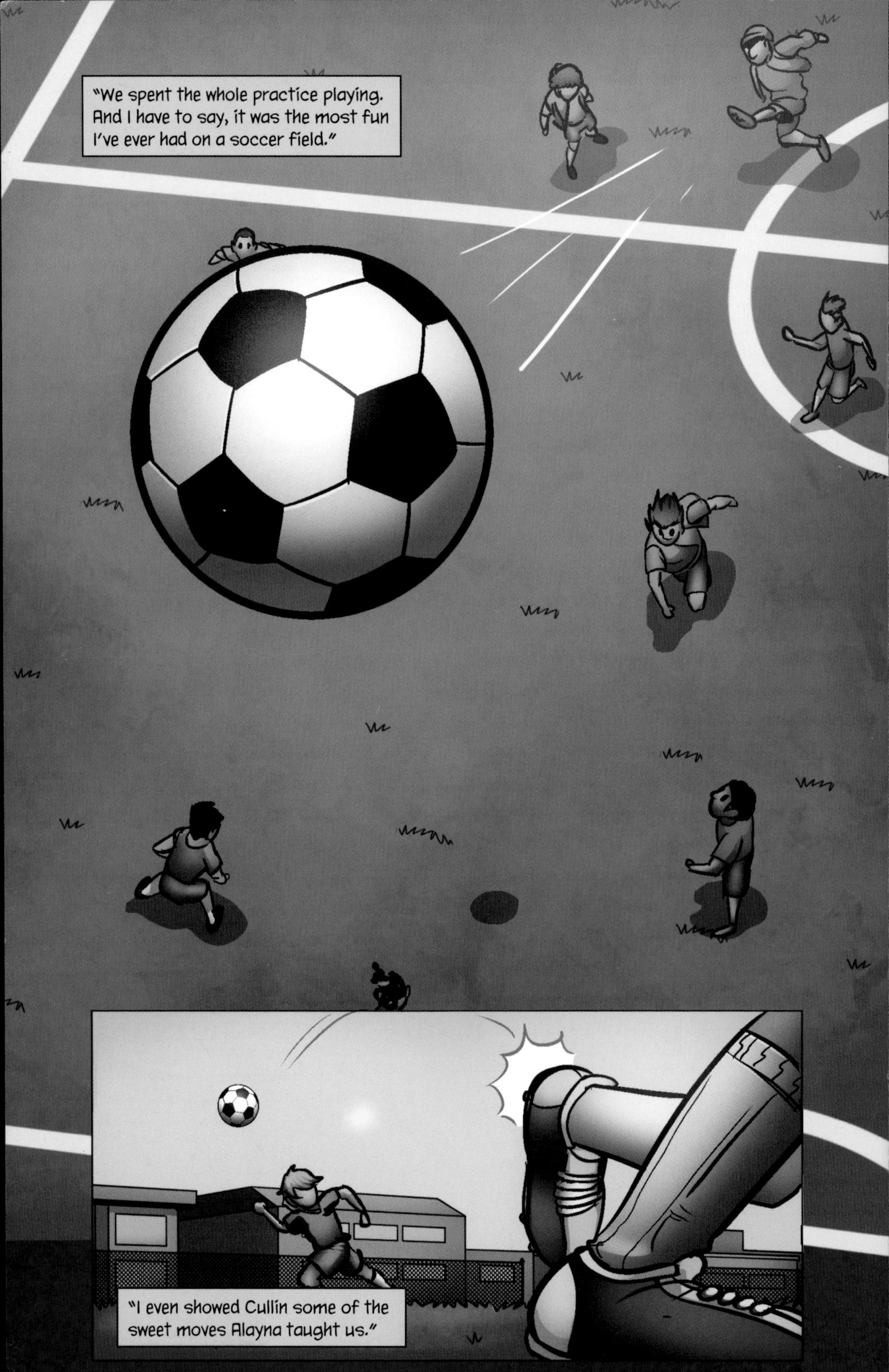
"We spent the whole practice playing. And I have to say, it was the most fun I've ever had on a soccer field."
"I even showed Cullin some of the sweet moves Alayna taught us."

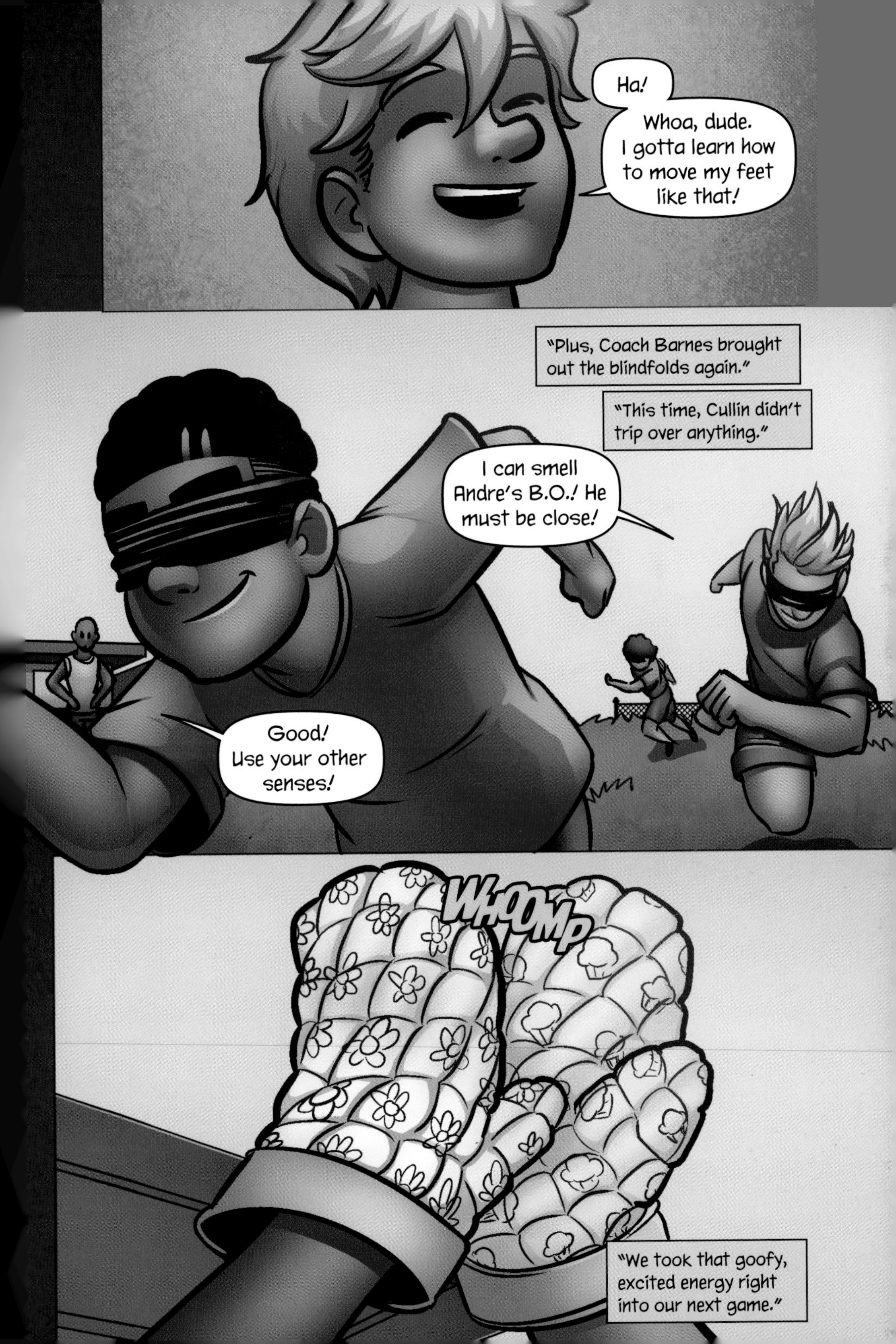
Ha!
Whoa, dude. I gotta learn how to move my feet like that!
"Plus, Coach Barnes brought out the blindfolds again."
"This time, Cullin didn't trip over anything."
I can smell Andre's B.O.! He must be close!
Good! Use your other senses!
WHOOMP
"We took that goofy, excited energy right into our next game."

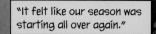

"It felt like our season was starting all over again."

"We were pumped up and ready to show off our new skills."

I've got a guy coming up fast! I can hear him!

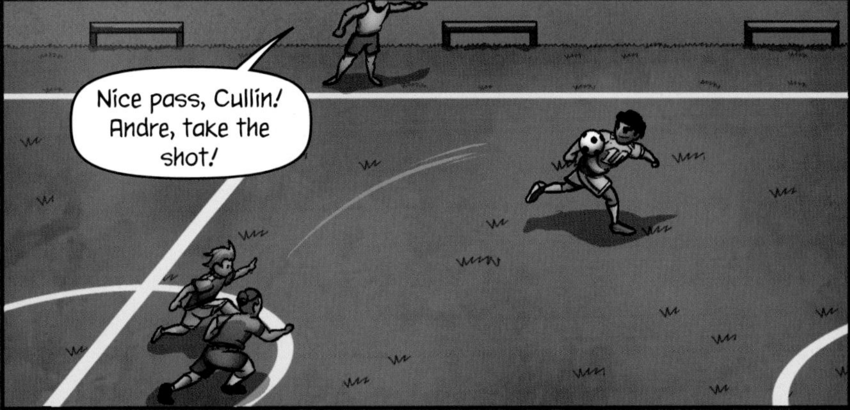
Nice pass, Cullin! Andre, take the shot!

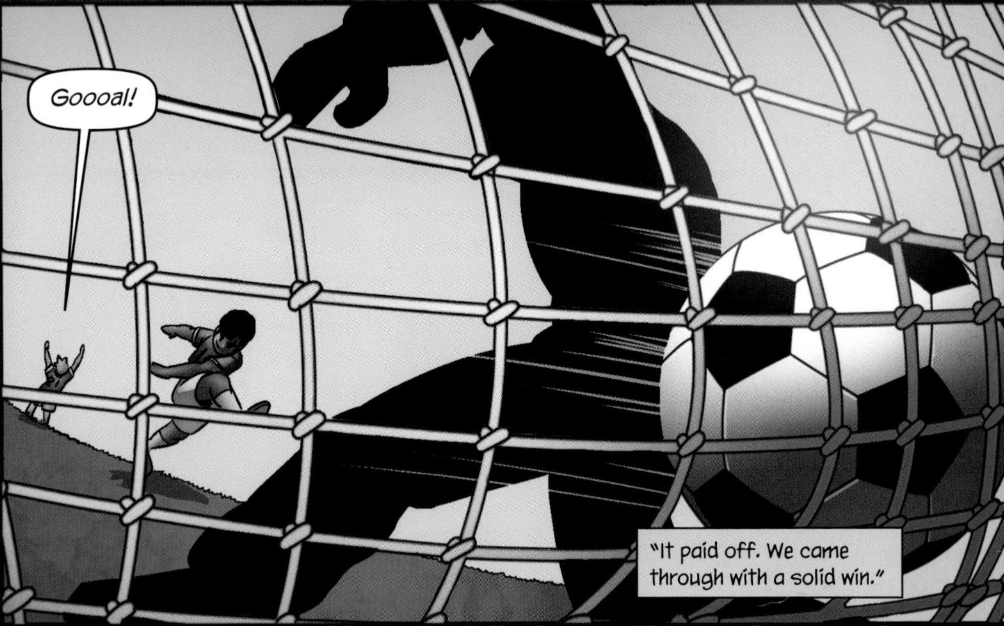
Goooal!
"It paid off. We came through with a solid win."

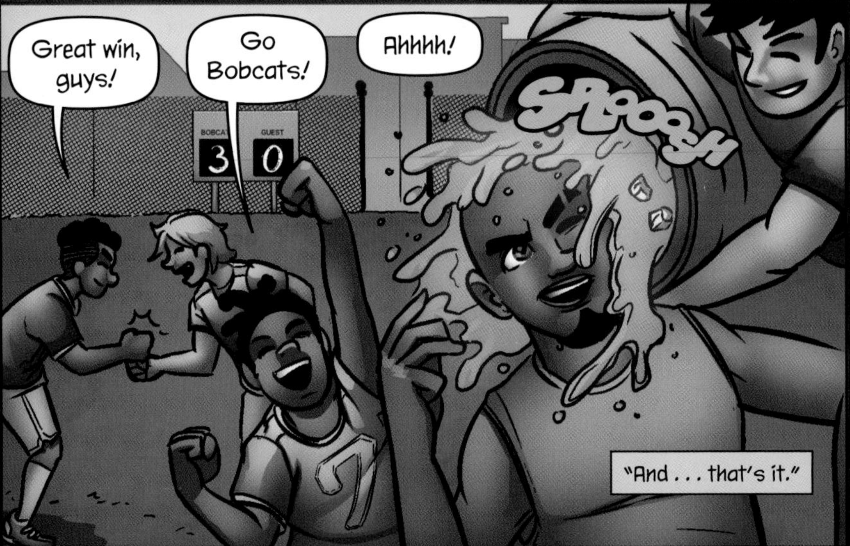
Great win, guys!
Go Bobcats!
Ahhhh!
SPLOOSH
"And . . . that's it."

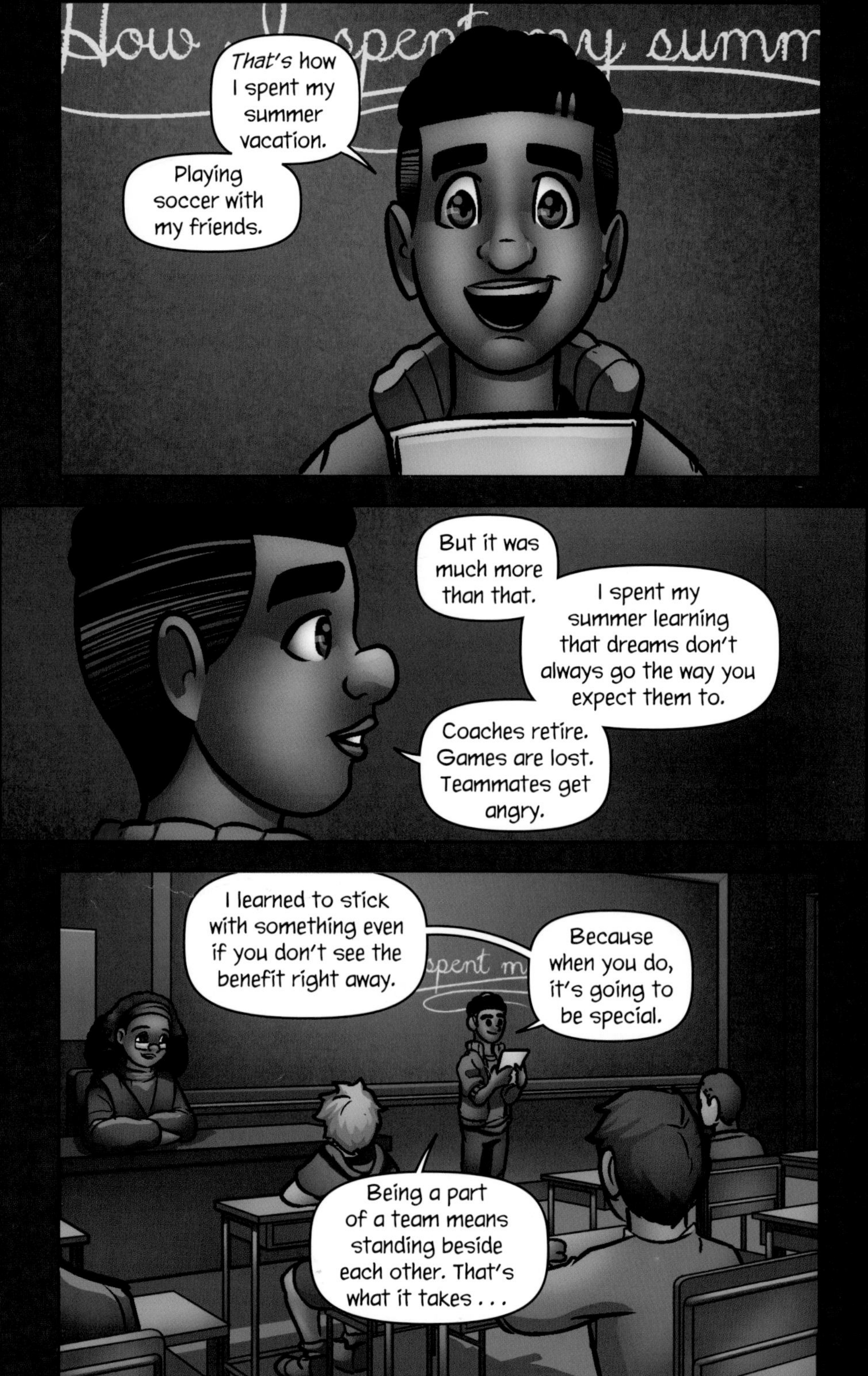
How I spent my summ
That's how I spent my summer vacation.
Playing soccer with my friends.
But it was much more than that.
I spent my summer learning that dreams don't always go the way you expect them to.
Coaches retire. Games are lost. Teammates get angry.
I learned to stick with something even if you don't see the benefit right away.
Because when you do, it's going to be special.
Being a part of a team means standing beside each other. That's what it takes . . .

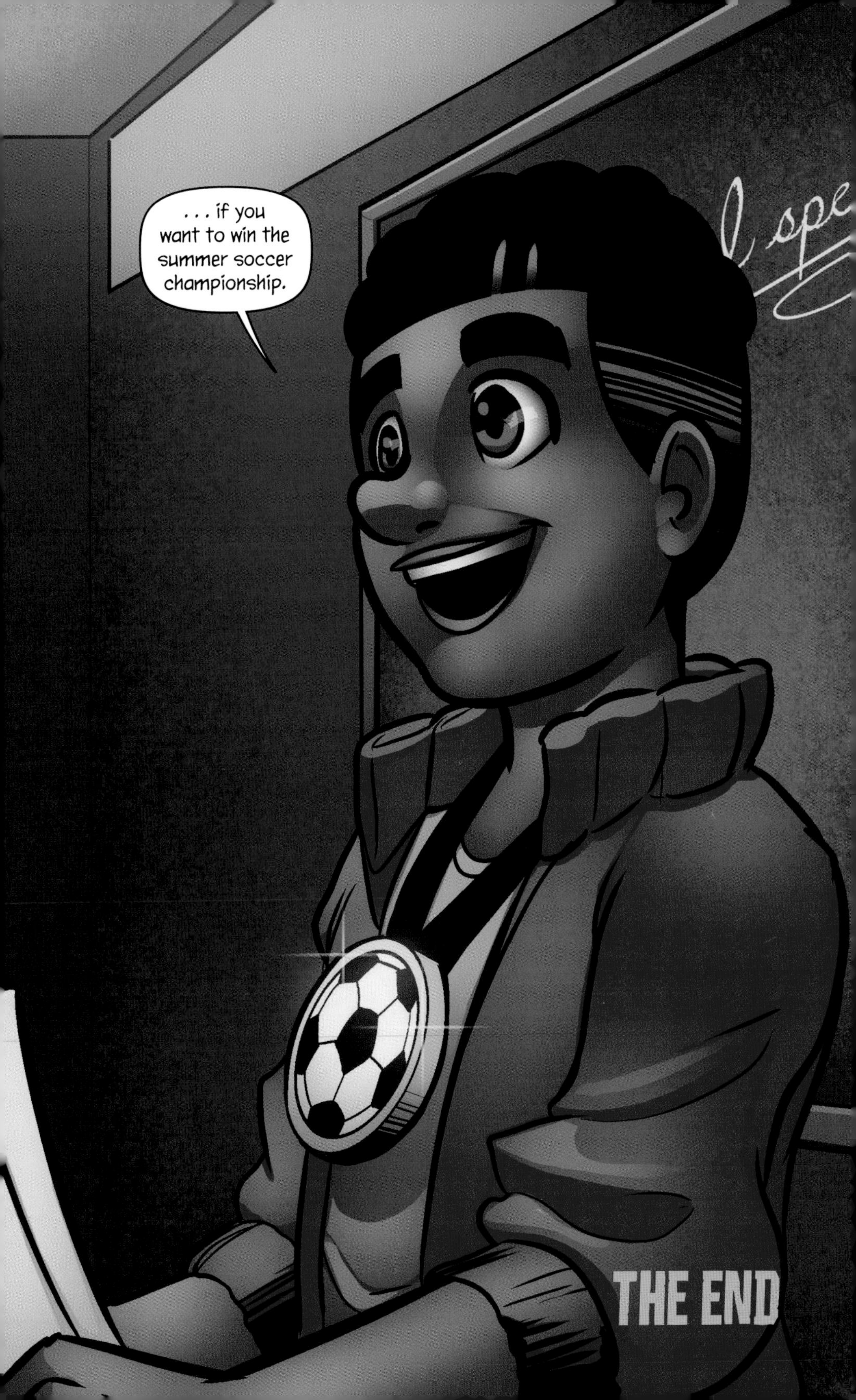
. . . if you want to win the summer soccer championship.
THE END

VISUAL QUESTIONS

Truth. The new guy better not pull another stunt like that, or my season is gonna be pretty dang short.

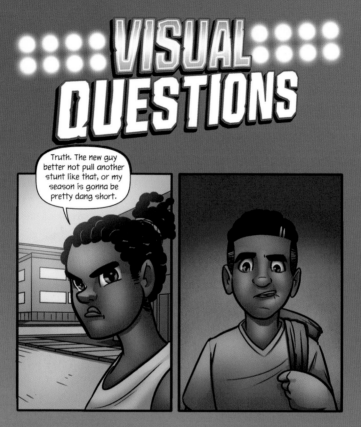

1. Andre doesn't reply after Cullin and Taye say how upset they are about practice and the new coach. But with graphic novels, you can often figure out what a character is thinking through his facial expression. What does Andre's expression tell you? What might he be thinking?

2. Why are some panels completely black during the blindfold drill? How does not seeing anything help you understand what the players are experiencing?

Here goes nothing.
"And 'nothing' was exactly what I saw."
"Not a single thing."
OK, let's run down the field. Stop on my command.
Run? You expect us to *run* in these?

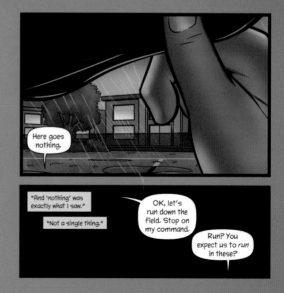

3. Why is Cullin upset? Look back through the story and write down three reasons he's feeling frustrated.

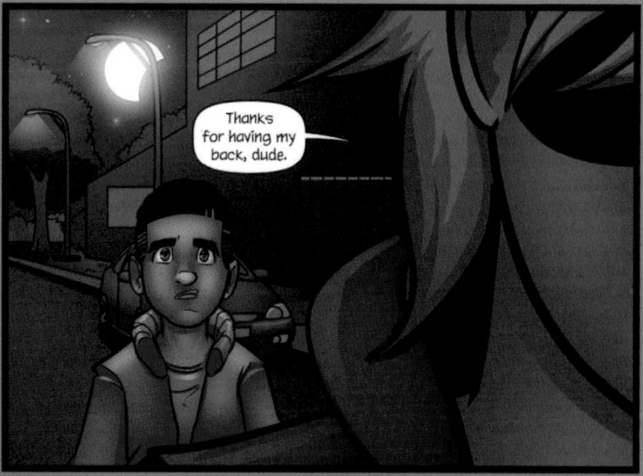
Thanks for having my back, dude.

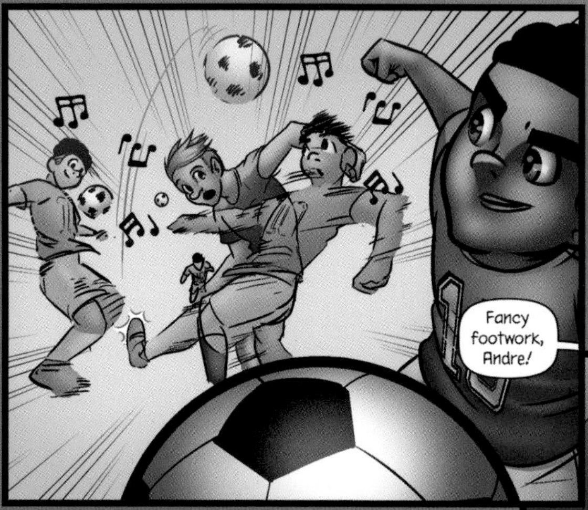
Fancy footwork, Andre!

4. Describe what's happening in this panel. Why is Andre shown four times in one panel? Talk about your answer.

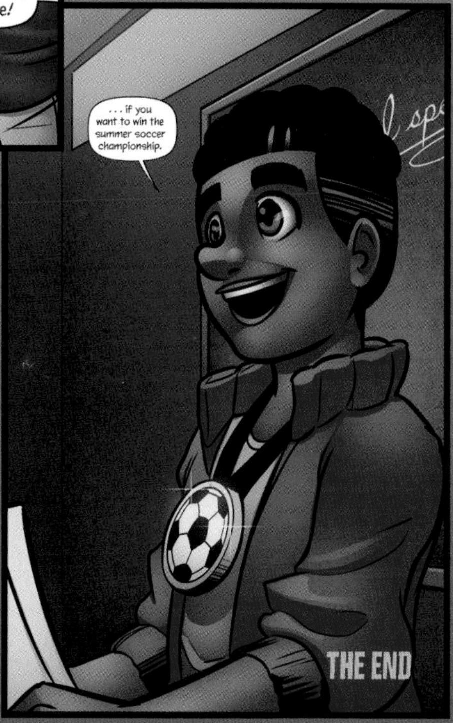
. . . if you want to win the summer soccer championship.
THE END

5. What is Andre wearing around his neck? Were you surprised by the ending? In your own words, write a paragraph about how the team was able to turn their season around and come out champions.

ALL-STAR SOCCER MOVES

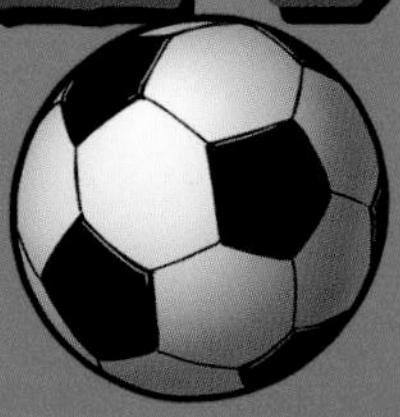

Ready to up your game? Soccer — or football, as it's known to most of the world — requires coordination, control, and speed. Read on to learn about advanced techniques that'll challenge your skills. Remember, practice is key to perfecting any new move!

CRUYFF TURN

Beat a defender with this classic turn. Put one foot to the side of the ball. Reach around the ball with your other foot. Stop the ball briefly with the inside of your foot. Pull the ball back. Turn and start dribbling in the other direction. First used by Dutch soccer player Johan Cruyff in the 1970s, this turn is still a popular dribbling skill.

RONALDO CHOP

Try out a signature move from famous Portuguese soccer pro Cristiano Ronaldo. As you're dribbling, take a small hop over the ball with both feet. Bring one foot down in front of the ball. Use the inside of your other foot to kick the ball as you land. Be sure to angle your foot at 45 degrees so you tap the ball forward. The sudden change in direction is perfect for throwing off a charging defender.

RAINBOW

Send the ball flying in an arc over your opponent. Use your dominant foot to roll the ball up the back of your other leg. Lean forward and quickly flick the ball with your non-dominant heel. At the same time, bring your dominant foot forward to help you land. Do all steps in one quick motion. The ball should pop up over you in a high curve. Keep running forward to recover the ball when it lands.

CHIP

Use this kicking technique to send the ball curving up into the air. As you approach the ball, plant one foot to the side of the ball. Swing your other leg back. A shorter swing will give you more control over the ball. Point your toes and bring your foot under the ball. Scoop the ball up and launch it into the air. The chip is good for passing, getting the ball past opponents, and tricking the goalie.

BENDING KICK

Curve the ball in midair with this expert kick. Approach the ball at an angle. Plant one foot to the side of the ball. Strike the ball with the inside of your other foot. Start at the bottom corner of the ball, and kick up and around it. Be sure to finish with your shoulders pointed in the direction you want the ball to travel. Use the bend to pass around an opponent or for shots on goal.

GLOSSARY

determination (di-tur-muh-NEY-shuhn)—the quality or act of continuing to try do something and not giving up, even though it may be difficult

drill (DRIL)—a repetitive exercise that helps you learn a specific skill

embarrassment (em-BAR-uhss-muhnt)—something or someone that causes you or a group to feel uncomfortable and foolish in front of others

experience (ik-SPIHR-ee-uhnss)—knowledge or skill gained from doing something

frustrations (fruh-STREY-shuhnz)—feelings of anger and annoyance because of something not going as planned or not being able to do something

humiliated (hyoo-MIL-ee-ate-ed)—made to feel ashamed and foolish

instincts (IN-stingktz)—behaviors that you don't have to think about in order to do

legend (LEJ-uhnd)—a person who is famous for doing something very well

retire (ri-TIRE)—to stop doing an activity or working a job, often because of old age

ridiculous (ri-DIK-yuh-luhss)—extremely silly and against common sense

scrimmage (SKRIM-ij)—a practice game between members of the same team

virtues (vir-CHOOZ)—very good qualities or features

READ THEM ALL!

JAKE MADDOX
GRAPHIC NOVELS
COMEBACK CATCHER

JAKE MADDOX
GRAPHIC NOVELS
DAYDREAM RECEIVER

JAKE MADDOX
GRAPHIC NOVELS
DOUBLE SCRIBBLE

JAKE MADDOX
GRAPHIC NOVELS
SOCCER SWITCH

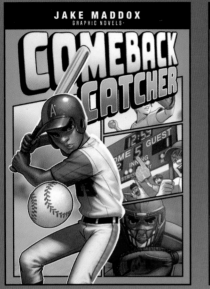

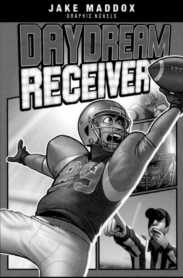

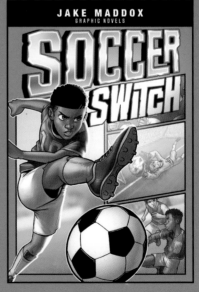

ABOUT THE AUTHOR

Brandon Terrell is the author of numerous children's books, including six volumes in the Tony Hawk's 900 Revolution series and several Sports Illustrated Kids Graphic Novels. When not hunched over his laptop writing, Brandon enjoys watching movies, reading, watching and playing baseball, and spending time with his wife and two children in Minnesota.

ABOUT THE ILLUSTRATOR

Aburtov has worked in the comic book industry for more than eleven years. In that time, he has illustrated popular characters such as Wolverine, Iron Man, Blade, and the Punisher. Recently, Aburtov started his own illustration studio called Graphikslava. He lives in Monterrey, Mexico, with his daughter, Ilka, and his beloved wife. Aburtov enjoys spending his spare time with family and friends.